MARTIN DASCOMB'S
CIVIL WAR

Ralph F. Leonard

Black Rose Writing | Texas

©2020 by Ralph F. Leonard
All rights reserved. No part of this book may be reproduced, stored in a retrieval system or transmitted in any form or by any means without the prior written permission of the publishers, except by a reviewer who may quote brief passages in a review to be printed in a newspaper, magazine or journal.

The author grants the final approval for this literary material.

First printing

This is a work of fiction. Names, characters, businesses, places, events, and incidents are either the products of the author's imagination or used in a fictitious manner. Any resemblance to actual persons, living or dead, or actual events is purely coincidental.

ISBN: 978-1-68433-574-9
PUBLISHED BY BLACK ROSE WRITING
www.blackrosewriting.com

Printed in the United States of America
Suggested Retail Price (SRP) $16.95

Martin Dascomb's Civil War is printed in Chaparral Pro

*As a planet-friendly publisher, Black Rose Writing does its best to eliminate unnecessary waste to reduce paper usage and energy costs, while never compromising the reading experience. As a result, the final word count vs. page count may not meet common expectations.

For Cathie

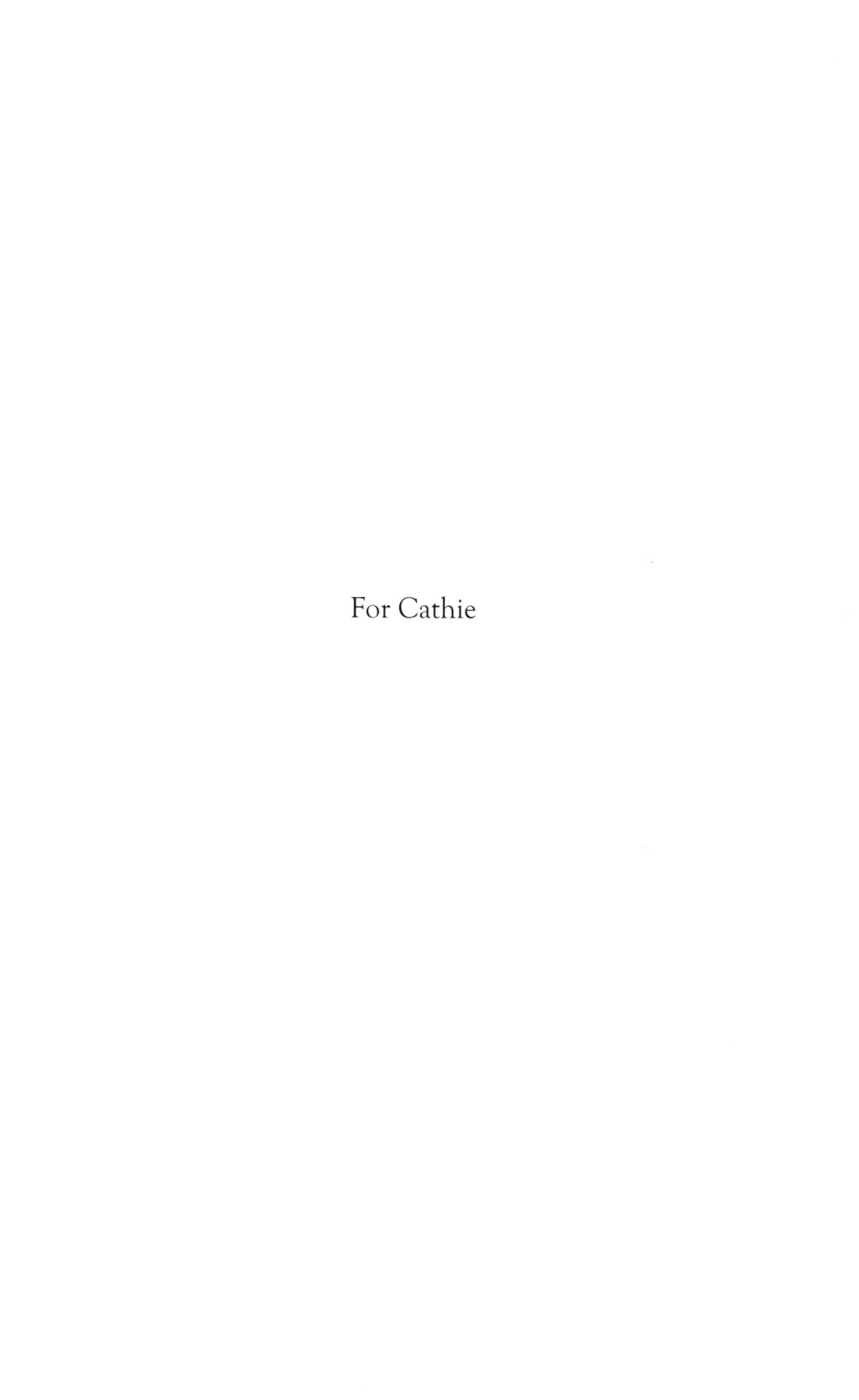

"It is not upon you alone the dark patches fall,
The dark threw down patches upon me also."
— Walt Whitman

MARTIN DASCOMB'S
CIVIL WAR

May 17, 1963

Hey Will,

    We found these old notebooks by a guy with your middle name and we thought you guys ought to have them. They were in a chest up in Gramps barn but he couldn't remember anything. I said I'd write a quick note but I think my mom's going to call about it.

    So anyway, it's not that long till the 4th of July and I'm starting to get psyched for running bases and bombing the sandpits like last year. So DO NOT forget your bike. How about seeing if we can stay a week up at Gram and Gramp's after the picnic? Talk to your mom about it, okay?

    I gained about an inch this year but not as much as you I bet.

    Lots of love (ha ha),
    Dan

ONE

The Tuesday afternoon pastors' meeting ended earlier than usual, and on the way home I stopped into Mr. Goodspeed's bookstore for a browse. I was but a few steps inside when my eye caught on the cover of the writing tablet now before me. The image is of an open hillside at daybreak as the first pink and orange rays creep into the tawny colors below. An ancient pine stands in silhouette on the crest. It was an ordinary slope, much as it might appear in New England after the last April snows have melted, and just the kind of farmland I had worked or passed by most every day in my years before coming to the city, But what struck me was the moment of emergence captured here, the poise between darkness and light, between old growth and new. I lingered, then drew away and started off. But halted.

Take it and begin!

I put the notebook on my account. And here I sit now, at my desk having gazed out the window for several minutes wondering why I'm still not settled with all that happened back then? Have I not come to terms with what my brother did? And my father's nature, and everything Mama endured? And Isis! I see her in the dark in the hayloft, with all her shorn hair in a heap beside her. And those first midnight steps out the door! I yearn for something, something that passed me by back then, mostly, and still escapes me. Understanding? Love?

From the pulpit I have spoken of love and how difficult and sometimes even frightening it can be, once likening it to looking at the sun or into the face of God. I have spoken of true love as a matter of attention far more than it is mere feeling, attention that asks us to be there with others. Fully and beyond ourselves.

But when I think of myself as I was a decade ago, still a few months shy of my fourteenth birthday and utterly absorbed in myself, perhaps I might be forgiven for lacking the capacity I've described. In 1863 I was thin, gangly, awkward, and self-conscious; not so different from my peers, though in intellectual pursuits I had long since developed beyond them, which was both a blessing and a curse. I had heard myself called "smart" and "thoughtful," even if it wasn't always meant as a compliment, and perhaps that aspect subjected me to more confusion than most by the ordinary actions of peers and adults.

And of course, those were not ordinary times. In July of 1863 everyone in New Hampshire, as elsewhere, was caught up in the events of a raging war; at home we certainly were, with my brother and only sibling away in the army and in the thick of the fighting. And while the war didn't bring it about, it took the lid off the family trouble that had simmered for several years before. And that summer, too, I saw my friend Isis' girlhood fall to pieces around her.

• • •

By the end of June, the two big armies had come tramping up out of Virginia, all strung out and tracking one another on opposite sides of a range of hills. Talk of a rebel invasion swirled about the village green at home.

Heard they're into Pennsylvania, by Jim!
Yep. Comin' after us up here, now!
Imagine them fellas. Invadin' us!
Nope. And wouldn't sprize me to see ol' Bob Lee boast right on into D.C. itself!

The war had not been going well, and indeed it was now at a most critical pass.

My brother had been two years with the Army of the Potomac. He had come safely through three engagements—with just the one minor scare: the time a minié ball nicked him on a forearm, a blow he described in typical humor in a letter shortly after as having wounded his coat sleeve considerably more than himself. But mostly he'd stayed healthy and out of trouble, and he remained satisfied with his lot in serving "Old Abe" and the Union's cause. He had also been promoted that spring. He was now *Lieutenant* Dascomb of Company G in the Second New Hampshire Infantry.

Twelve years stood between Ned and me, We were Mama's only two, though there'd been another, a girl of three who had died a number of years before I was born. With Father then, we were three on the farm in Greenfield at the time. Our story and a half clapboard house stood on gently rising land a hundred yards above the Contoocook River. It faced across the road to the larger cow barn, and upwards beyond to our wide pastureland. The barn and house were like separate centers—male and female hubs, as you might say. They were only fifty feet apart, but divided by the road that ran between Peterborough, eight miles to the south, and our own, smaller village a few miles farther along to the north. The barn looked smart, having been freshly red-washed, while the house, with its skin cracked and dulled to grey, waited its turn.

Father maintained a herd of twenty cows. In the morning and again in late afternoon we drew milk and kept it on ice in heavy steel cans that were picked up twice a week and taken to Manchester, from where much of it went down to Boston. By six or seven I'd been given small tasks about the house and barn, with increasing responsibilities as I grew. As for Mama, it would be accurate to say that she hardly ever sat down, at least not to any leisure; and with times as hard as they were then, she regularly took on barn and greater garden chores in addition to her usual labors. She was of medium height, stout, energetic, and as hearty as most any male. So far as I knew Mama had never been sick a day in her life—or if so, she never let on. My father was wiry strong and taller than most men, yet still four inches shorter than Ned. In both movement and thought he was deliberate.

I was an able scholar, and in recent years at school I had been given considerable freedom to read and pursue studies of my own. But in June, only two weeks before the summer session was set to begin, we lost our teacher to the war. Ned's good friend, Thomas Partridge, had made an abrupt decision to go home and join a Vermont regiment. Mr. Partridge was most appropriately nicknamed Sunbeam, and every now and then some of us even smiled it out loud to his face. He suggested readings, found me books and gave me extra time to discuss them, and perhaps in return he felt free to rely on me for help with his other charges, all but one or two of whom appreciated me as an able assistant.

Sunbeam's departure put my privileged status in jeopardy, and I grew increasingly anxious as a replacement for him was sought, and soon found, so that the beginning of our summer session was postponed only two days. Word went quickly round that a woman would be coming up - and from Boston, no less! My worries, as it would turn out, were not ill founded.

• • •

The morning of July second came in bright and dry and even a bit cool as we twenty or so scholars mounted schoolhouse hill and waited, shifting about below the granite doorstone. Some of us, or most, kept tight faces, while two or three of the older fellows made a show of disdainful nonchalance.

At last came a sharp snap at the latch and the heavy door swung open to a blank-faced, big-shouldered woman dressed in black silk. Out she thrust herself to stand erect and glaring out over our heads into the distance!

My heart thumped.

She lowered her head to fix, then fiercely address us.

"Line UP! GIRLS. FIRST! No boys!"

We stood like stone posts

"NOW! And be quick about it!"

Her name was Miss Wood, and it wasn't long til it struck me as fitting her as fully as Sunbeam's nickname had fit him.

The morning passed quietly. Every voice, when any were required, came meekly and exaggeratedly polite. We were granted no movement about, and once, then again, our Mistress looked up to discourage even a squeaky bench. By the time she dismissed us for the noon recess we were all of us coiled springs.

I went off with the older boys to our customary spot under the big chestnut, where we volleyed back and forth in consternation, then emptied our lunch pails and charged off down the hill to play ball on the field below.

We were seven boys, and Isis, who came along when invited to even the sides. She was never picked first, even if we all understood she should have been, and everyone, including me, resented that she was the most agile among us. Isis often ended up teamed with me—and the two us rarely with Scoonie Fenn, who might have disliked her even more than he did me.

I had chummed with Isis for years, even if days, sometimes weeks went by when she didn't come down from the mountain. She had been a true friend, and truth to say, my closest. I was drawn to the quiet and self-contained way of her, though she was anything but bashful. She was decidedly not school smart and lagged beyond any of us learning to read; yet she cared not, nor did she hold it against me as some did that I was so bookish. Her surpassing intelligence was elemental. She listened. She touched. She watched. By the age of seven or eight she could follow a bee to its hive. She told me that if you went early in the morning and were careful, you could go into the comb using a thin stick. But the bees could tell if you were afraid, she said, so you had to go in just natural.

"Imagine yourself like one of them," she said.

"Oh sure!" I said.

She showed a great interest in horses and always went to our two whenever she'd come to the farm. Father let her climb up or walk them about now and then. He noticed their ease with her, and she told him she watched their heads and especially their ears for how they felt. Father told me afterward that it was wasted on Isis that she wasn't a boy.

Isis was just my age—her birthday eleven days after mine in November—and we were about the same height, though she had already begun to grow into herself and I had not. My nut-brown hair - brown as a monk's robe, Ned had once called it - was thin and a wavy, hers thick, course. and ink-black. I was pale eight months of the year, while Isis kept her brownish hue the whole year round. But most distinctive were her large, dark eyes set back under a thickly-lashed brow. These, in their often steady gaze, quite put me in mind of an owl. She had been born in California of an Indian father and a mother who had been a circus performer, a horsewoman - before a fall that had left her brain-damaged. She had never known her father or anything about him other than his name. Graywind!

If Isis's mother was enfeebled, the reclusive man she lived with—"NOT my stepfather", as she insisted—was almost equally unknowable. To most everyone he was at best Mr. Croslin, but just as often spoken of as "that fellow." Isis called him Claude. He had brought them to New Hampshire when she was still a toddler to live on the far outskirts of town, on the western slope of Butternut Mountain where few townspeople had ventured. I'd heard their dwelling described as a poor shanty in a hacked-out clearing, surrounded by a few chickens, a milk cow, an old mare.

I have written about not seeing Isis for long stretches. But whenever she appeared on schoolhouse hill, it was always in one of two faded, threadbare gowns. Often she brought only bread and butter for lunch, sometimes only the bread. Most days she'd stay about the village for a time after school, and we'd always pick up as if there'd been no break. But in the last year, as we became increasingly aware of ourselves in new ways, Isis and I had begun to grow apart; and increasingly I felt the need to prove myself against the sniggering comments of the boys. Which brings to mind an incident that mortified me more than any other before or since.

Several months earlier a surge of emotion had overwhelmed me. I grabbed her by the shoulders and pulled her in to smother her face with my own. She jerked herself away and gave me a sharp slap, and then some harsh words before running off.

But now, to the ball field on that singular day. July 2nd. The game had gone on for the better part of the lunch hour when Isis came to the bat for the third or fourth time. I stood behind her, serving as both catcher and umpire, and she sent Alf's first pitch straight back past his ear. Jerry lunged and snagged the ball splendidly off its bounce. He staggered and almost fell, but righted himself to peg a line to Scoonie, who swiped at Isis as she crossed the base. The field erupted.

"Out!"

"Oh yeah, got her!"

"She's OUT!"

Isis turned and looked out at the field. "He missed me."

"Did not!" Scoonie howled.

Another broadside from the field, and then a short silence.

"Rule on it, Dascomb!" Scoonie demanded.

Another silence.

"Aw-w, look," said Jerry, my sometime friend. "He's still sweet on her, ain't that right, Marty?" Ripples of laughter, "I said ain't that right, Marty!" My face flushed hot. I spun away with. My chest heaved. A half mile away the church steeple gleamed like a raised sword above the treetops. Alf called in to take it over.

"Wha-duhya say?" said Scoonie after a moment.

Scoonie had missed her by at least six inches. I knew it, he knew it. Maybe we all did!

"How 'bout it, Pro-FESSER," Scoonie mocked. "You decide."

Decide. Decide on one trouble. Or another. Trouble from them. Trouble with myself. But mostly *her* and what she'd think!

I drew a deep breath. "Sure," I muttered, then turned back and hollered "Sure! Take it over."

I kept my eyes from Isis. I felt weak and ashamed, but when the sides changed and Jerry trotted by and murmured something else about Isis, I erupted, lost myself and leapt at him. Jerry went down hard under me. We wrestled up and kept at it in a flurry of fists and limbs. But I had the advantage of all my bitter disgust at all of them and at myself, and I took it out on poor Jerry. I pinned him to the hardpack and ground at the side of his head.

All at once the din broke off.

Someone cried out. "Jesus! It's HER!"

Hands yanked at me. "Hey, Marty! Hey!"

And so the fight ended. Or one did. Within minutes the scrap was all but forgotten.

As we marched up the hill before Miss Wood's menacing stick, the Cowell twins returned from lunch at home and began calling from the road below.

"The fightin's begun! It's begun down there!"

. . .

For the next hour Jerry and I stood side by side up front with our backs to the class and orders to keep 'nose and toes' to the wall; but my humiliation was quickly dispelled by images of Ned and other men in blue somewhere in Pennsylvania hundreds of miles away.

I raced home later, and not long after Father returned from the village to report that the two armies were fully drawn in and that the fighting had in fact started the day before. He quoted the latest dispatch reporting the New Hampshire men as "heavily engaged." It was precisely how we felt, too, heavily engaged, just as we had several times before while waiting for word from Fredericksburg, from Chantilly and several other battles, and dreading the arrival of the casualty lists - and worst of all, the *names* that would sooner or later be wired in.

I had, of course, seen the covers of *Leslie's* and *Harper's Weekly* with its sketches of men with bayonets forward charging on the double-quick at big guns belching smoke and flame, with officers waving swords behind on rearing horses. I ought to have been better by now at keeping my imagination at bay, but I was not. And as always before, I threw myself into my late day chores at a pace that at another time might have brought a compliment from Father.

At the supper table, I ate ravenously and with a haste that had Mama put down her fork to bid me slow down. Afterward, the two of us cleared the table. She began to wash and I to dry at her side, but almost at once her fingers fumbled at a dish and it nearly fell from us in the passing. She stopped and smiled at me sweetly.

"Now it's me needs to slow down," she said.

An hour later I headed out behind the house and scuffled along down the narrow path toward the river. The lowering sun ahead, looking larger and closer than usual, shimmered in the sultry air beyond the river. Grasshoppers jumped from the path just ahead. A crow barked insistently in the woodlot off to my left.

The Contoocook ran all along the western border of our property. As rivers go it wasn't much—never more than twenty feet across, but for me it was perfect. I had spent many an idle hour along its banks, in it, and on it in the winter. I knew its seasonal currents and all its shades and shifts of color. The black depths had once frightened me, but over the years even these had grown familiar.

Go down and take a dip for me, won't you Marty.

Ned had bid me this—wryly, as was his wont—toward the end of his latest letter that had arrived just the day before. It had been shorter than most, only three paragraphs on one side of a sky-blue sheet, and except for the one request above, it lacked anything of his usual lightness and humor. He said that they'd tramped forty-five miles in twenty-four hours and that in the terrible heat, three men of Company G had fallen out to sunstroke. But in a one-line last paragraph he sounded firm.

If this is a Rebel invasion, we mean to stop it.

I stood musing by the river's edge. We'd had some times down here, hadn't we, he and. I thought of his occasional challenges: Which of us would land the first breakfast trout? If it was me, he'd go on to another. Who'd take the biggest? Once, after the barn work was done and we were here on a steamy evening like this one, we had wrestled out of our sweat-soaked clothes and lazed about and let ourselves drift in the current til we were clear down by the covered bridge. But here it was me who surprised us both!

"Run through it, Neddy," I said. "Betcha can't." He scrunched up his face. We were both naked to the toes!

"You can't!" I taunted.

He looked at me a long moment "A challenge is it?" he said, breaking one of his sly grins. "All right then ... you first!"

"NO-O-O! Neddy, YOU!"

"My good young man. You breed it, you lead it!"

"Huh?"

"An old biblical saying, Mart," he said with a self-satisfied gleam. "It means you have to go first."

His eyes held mine. And held til I had to do *something*! I scanned the road up and down, found it empty, and then of a sudden found myself thrashing up and out and scrambling off. I kept up a desperate sprint and took the turn into the bridge to fix my eye on the gleaming square at the far end.

And then I was out. Out, and across, and leaping gleefully into the air.

"Now YOU, Neddy!"

I can hear now the slap of his big feet on the planks. I hear our laughter afterward and see the beam in his eye.

"See when I'll ever swim down here with *you* again," he said.

My special place by the river was where it began a broad sweep westward toward Mount Monadnock, ten miles away and visible to us as a low, blue hump. Here, only a few yards above the bank, was an eight-foot-wide granite boulder standing a hands breadth taller than Ned. It presented a broad flat face to the river, but its backside sloped at an angle that made it easy to mount even as a small boy. Years before I was born Ned had named this Secret Rock. About it we had fished and swam and conversed, but it was awhile before I thought to ask why he called it Secret. He'd looked at me askance, as if wondering how I didn't know. He said it was because the rock held lots of secrets.

"Awh, Neddy!"

"Hey! Whad'ya think makes it so heavy?"

"What secrets?" I scoffed.

"That ain't for us to find out, Mart. That's how come it's so blamed hard."

"Aww-h, Neddy."

He told me stories about Indians; he kept me spellbound, making me see painted faces and naked bodies whooping and dancing about.

"Oh, yes. It's true!" he said, waving a hand all around. "Right here, right where we're sitting now,"

He used to write in his notebooks down here, his poems and the like, and the last thing I remember him working up was on a glorious day in the spring of '62. His regiment had been sent back to New Hampshire on leave, clearly for political purposes, and here at the Rock Ned had labored on the speech he later gave in Concord and in several towns around us, urging votes for the Lincoln administration.

The Rock was like an ancient gray kin of the river itself, and in the last year, with Ned away in the army, both of these had come to feel almost grandfatherly, like two wise old men.

Before shucking out of my linens for Ned's dip, I stood by the rock and looked out toward the mountain. Ned's regiment and all the clashing hordes would be out that way, far beyond. I tugged hard at my shirt.

But then, with it up about my ears, I heard a call from some distance away. It sounded odd, thick, and it took a second to register that it was *me* being hailed! The voice came louder.

"Martin Das'um? Dat be you?"

I pulled my shirt down and searched out through the trees, then squinted to find a man forty or fifty yards away. Short, broad, wearing a straw hat. He raised an arm and started toward me, slowly and without speaking. And all at once I stiffened.

Coming on at me through our own south woodlot ···

A colored ... a Negro!

I hollered. "Hey, what're you up to here?" He halted. I repeated the demand. He stood still for several moments, then leaned to set down a carpetbag. He took off his hat. "Don't take no alarm," he said.

"I ain't taking no alarm; what do you want?"

"Jus need some help is all. Jus hopin' fo' de brother uf Ned Das'um."

With a finger you might have tipped me over.

"I come by here with somethin," he said a little louder now. "But dey say Ned's off wif de Union." I stood dumbfounded. "Ah'm a friend uf Ned, see," he said and pointed at his chest. "Robert. Dat's me." The voice was firm, yet kindly.

I had seen but one or two colored men in all my days, and never spoken to one. "Well we don't need nothin mister," I said, "so just go on with you."

He dipped his head and backed away a step.

"Hear me a minute now. See, down N'awluns onc't, down that way ah' knowed Ned an' now ah'm comin' to Boston an' join into da Union, too." He paused. "But dis letter ah' got, it's fo Ned. Back in town dey say give it to Misses Das'um,"

"What'! What you got?"

"Got dis letter. An' ah see'd you crossin dat field."

He rummaged about in his bag and held up an envelope.

"Ned shuly wan see dis!" he said

I stared at the envelope, then lifted my eyes. He was well kept in a clean linen shirt and a decent pair of trousers. He asked if could come on and show me what he had.

"You came here from ⋯ where? *New Orleans*?"

He smiled. "But ain't been there fo' some time, no suh." He began cautiously toward me while saying he'd been in Canada for two years. He said he'd known Ned from his teaching. "Yessir," he said. "Ned Das'um bout the fines' white man ah ever did know."

"What! How come?" I snapped, hearing only now how disagreeable I'd been.

He held up a hand and said, "Taught me to read, he did. Yes, suh!"

My brother had gone to New Orleans in 1859 shortly after graduating from Dartmouth College with a classmate who lived in that city. He had intended to stay for six months, hoping to understand more about the South and its ways, but he had returned, unexpected and unannounced, in less than two. One afternoon as I brought kindling into the kitchen I heard the familiar tromp of his boots come up on the porch. Ned admitted that he'd been asked to leave Louisiana after "doing a little work with the Negroes," but he never offered more—at least not to me.

"He taught you to read!" I asked, more softly now.

He nodded and said there was something else he wanted me to see. And while he went again into the cloth bag, I took in more. He was scarcely taller than me but very broad at the chest and hips. His face, not the coal black I would have expected, was instead a kind of polished chestnut brown.

He came on again and stopped a few feet away. His eyes were large and set sideways like almonds, and they gleamed proudly as he held up a black leather book not much larger than a deck of cards.

He opened the cover - and even as he held the pages out I felt a bolt!

The New Testament title scarcely registered, for my eyes caught at once on the right-leaning, black-ink script below.

Robert Smith's book. Presented as a token of friendship and respect, from Ned Dascomb. And below it, *In here will be much to guide you.*

I read through a second time after the shock withdrew. Then I went back to the words, *a token of friendship.*

I looked up in wonder.

"Yez suh, be sum troof in dat book," he said. "Ah have found dat so."

How had he met my brother? What had happened? Who sent him away? I asked these all together in a rush. But he turned it all away, politely, gently, only saying it would be Ned's to tell and that he had to get back. He brought out the letter and told me it was from someone Ned had known in New Orleans, someone who also now lived in Montreal. He said they'd both come north in the company of a family in the months before the war broke out.

His kindly look and quiet assurance, the way he stood and held himself, somehow even in so short a time had I turned to feel disposed toward him. I told him I'd forward the letter and then found myself offering him the barn loft for the night, knowing it would never do to take him to the house. He thanked me and said that before he'd left, his church had arranged a room with a family in Peterborough. In the morning he'd be going on to Boston.

Four or five steps out of the woods and under the open sky, I stopped and turned to gaze back into the trees. And I recall now the depth I had seen in Robert Smith's brown eyes and the impression that lingered in me.

I lay awake in bed that night with my head all awhirl: Ned in Pennsylvania, Ned in New Orleans; the Negro in the woodlot and the writing in his little book.

And the letter under my bed. Written by a woman! For it was clearly a woman's hand on the envelope.

I had come into the house and said nothing about the letter or its bearer; to do otherwise would have brought an unthinkable commotion.

TWO

It was common in our town and throughout southwest New Hampshire, as far as I knew, to think of Negroes as but partly human. Niggers, coloreds, spooks, jigaboos. All these were terms I had heard. I had laughed at the jokes and taken as much delight as anyone in the caricatures that appeared regularly on the pages of *Harper's Weekly* or *Leslie's*. I saw one that same night as I thrust myself yet again onto one side: a circle of grinning, bug-eyed black men high-stepping about in a barn, while another, seated among them on an overturned washtub, stroked a banjo with long, frantic fingers.

My brain also churned up an incident it had taken me days to get over, a time two years earlier on the day Ned returned from the village after enlisting in the Second. Father had been at work replacing a fence post a few rods up the road when Ned came down the rise. From the yard I watched as Father stood out and Ned brought the wagon to a halt. They exchanged a few words and then it turned harsh.

"And for *what*?" Father asked. "For niggers? Is that it?"

Ned turned a hardened face my way as Father pressed him.

"Get yerself killed for niggers! IS THAT RIGHT?"

I could feel the moment still before Ned whirled and jabbed an arm. Father reeled, stumbled, and dropped to his knees.

"That's part of it!" shouted Ned, stabbing a finger. "The rest is to rid the country of blamed fools like you!"

He turned and startled Chub with a vicious snap at the reins. The wagon came on at a clip, and I watched it past, past the house and barn, and into the bend to disappear beyond. I stood agape. In my brother I'd never seen the like of it. And when I turned back to Father, this, too, I'd never seen. He stood with his head down, looking helpless, almost boyish. I remember the surge of affection that rose in me. And it would be a long time til I felt similarly again.

• • •

In the morning I followed my heavy feet along to school, where I endured the hours in something of a daze. My stomach felt like lead. The mistress made no reference whatever to the battle she surely knew was on the minds of her charges. But there was one good thing: early on I looked at Jerry, he looked back at me, and our faces both said the same thing: that we were sorry for a scrape that felt like it had taken place in another world.

That afternoon passers-by at home brought word of the latest dispatches telling of "heavy casualties" and "continued fighting into a third day," As yet, no news of the four New Hampshire units.

It was July third, and with Independence Day on the morrow, Mama should have been full of bustle and cheer as she readied herself for the coming festivities. Not today, not with this now our third or fourth time of agonized waiting after a battle. Rain helped put me to sleep that night but awakened me later when it came down hard for a time.

Father attempted a little cheer when he came into the kitchen the following morning. He said it was beginning to clear and should be a "passable day" after all. He looked my way and proposed that the two of us have a go at the horseshoe tournament later. I dipped my head away.

"Might be a little muddy in the pits," he said, "but they'll bring in some sand." And with some of the men staying down to the telegraph office, he thought we'd stand a good chance at a ribbon. "Well, we'll see," he said when I offered only a weak look in response.

Father turned his attention to Mama, at work on the picnic basket behind me. "They're expecting quite a crowd up to Concord today, Lucy," he said. Mama returned silence. "Ten, twenty thousand I hear," he said. Still, nothing. Father tried again. "Don't s'pose you know the attraction, do ya?"

Mama sighed and said simply, "Frank Pierce,"

"Ayuh. And that man ain't spoken in years. Nope. Not once since he got out of office I'd wager, what do you make of *that*?"

"I don't make a thing of it," Mama said and started toward the pantry. "Can't say as I blame him none," she murmured as she withdrew.

Franklin Pierce was a one-term President who had left office in some disgrace. He had been Mama's childhood neighbor in Hillsborough, fifteen miles to the north, and at another time she'd have stopped to engage in anything positive about "Frankie," as she spoke of him.

"Well, he's gonna get a warm reception today," Father called after. "I heard he's making the case against fighting this war any futher. And I tell ya', there's a whole lot of folks want to hear it."

Indeed, My father was one of them. He'd been against the war from the beginning. He had even supported secession.

. . .

We left the farm for Peterborough at 9:00. Puddles mottled the road ahead. The sun had risen half high, and like a big yellow-white wafer, it glowed through a thinning cloud-cover. Mama passed the first miles silent and brooding. Always before she had made up a new dress, or at least bought herself a new bonnet, but she had dressed herself in a brown-and-black-striped gown and a tan bonnet, both of which I'd seen regularly for a while. Her hair was up in the usual pins, but strands of it hung loosely, fluttering about her neck. All at once my heart lurched. I put out a hand to her shoulder, and she reached back to cover it with her own.

Before long we turned onto the main road from Concord and Hillsboro that led south into Peterborough. Our pace slowed as we fell in with a growing number of wagons and folks afoot. I wondered about Robert Smith coming down this same road only the night before. Some might have offered him a ride, some would have looked him over in silence and passed by; but I knew of one or two who would surely have stopped him short.

Where you going, friend? What're you up to?

Father tipped his Sunday straw hat forward. He had freshly shaved, and I could see the inch-long boyhood scar on his cheek below one ear.

My father was fifty-four years old then, nine years older than Mama. He and Ned were both sinewy and long-limbed, and they walked with the same long strides, with their arms swinging along beside them in wide arcs that came naturally but looked embellished (and to me at times a little comical). In appearance they were similar, and they both enjoyed a strain of sardonic humor, but otherwise the two were almost entirely different.

Father had a hard-set mind about most things; he simply *knew* how things were or should be. And so now, when I decided it was as good a time as any to carefully ask about Negroes, I knew what to expect. I leaned forward.

"Father, are any Negroes living around here?"

His head tipped back sharply.

"What's that?" he said. I repeated it.

"Well ... there'd be one over to Jaffrey, I guess. What brings it up?"

"I heard some of them are going into the army," I said.

"Ayuh," he said over his shoulder. "Where'd you hear? That new teacher, is it?"

"Just some of the boys," I said.

"Uh-huh. Well ... there's a couple of Negro outfits now, that's true. Lincoln wants to put 'em to use, I guess."

"I just wondered if they'd help much, that's all."

"Sure they will. Long as they've got regular officers to lead 'em."

I thought for a moment. "Anyway, I guess they're pretty different from us."

"Well, no, they ain't," he said. "Not in most ways. Only a little lower in the order of things, is all. But no, they have some attributes."

Mama shifted somewhat uneasily on the bench, and I took the cue and sat back to the steady return of Chub's hooves. A minute passed but then Father continued.

"Ya see," he said, leaning back, "there's a reason there ain't many Negroes hereabouts. They don't take much to cold winters."

"But I ain't cared for them either," I blurted, then winced.

Mama turned to throw me glare,

"Sam," she said a few moments later, "that house we passed just now, it's been painted, ain't it? Didn't it used to be yellow?"

"Could be," Father said curtly. He slowed Chub a little. And then returned to me.

"Those fellows prefer it down south where it's nice and hot," he said. "I guess they're like fish out of water up here."

I saw Robert Smith. And once again the impulse overtook me. "But we aren't fish out of water down *there*!" I said.

Mama's shoulders tightened. The wheels churned beneath us. Father looked straight out ahead.

"Well, that's just one of the differences, ain't it!" he said.

• • •

Peterborough gathered itself around four or five streets in a shallow valley where another Abenaki-named river ran into the Contoocook. This was the region's commercial center, but its chief distinction was having established some thirty years earlier the nation's first free and publicly supported library.

We came onto Main Street at late morning and began up a gentle slope between the shops and churches. On the crest to the right stood the brick schoolhouse, and beyond, the road narrowed to wander off among the highland farms. The boardwalks were already crowded. Knots of men and women stood by chattering; children chased about in the throng. And everything had been decked out in red-white-and-blue. Flags hanging limp on six-foot stakes lined both sides, storefronts were draped in patriotic bunting. The air was bright and warm, and on the surface it all looked usual and perfect for the occasion.

One of Mama's friends came off the planks toward us, one hand hailing, the other clutching her skirts. "Lucy, I been looking for you," she said fervently, with a touch of concern. "Oh my!" Mama muttered aside. Mrs. S reached out a hand. "We are all praying," she said. Mama thanked her. She said we were praying, too.

But I had not prayed! I had not prayed for some time, not for a year perhaps, and it had almost ceased to trouble me.

Prayer had always come hard. Father had required it of me twice daily beginning as early as my fifth year. And I had tried; morning after morning, night upon night I had knelt by my bed. But God never answered me, and I never sensed His presence, as Father said I would. I blamed myself: I hadn't been good enough, or sincere about my sins. And by then I'd begun hearing Ned's heated responses to Father, telling how God wasn't to be found mainly in the pages of a book and the like.

One day Ned had stunned me with this: "There's more than one God in our Bible, Father. And I don't believe in the one you've chosen." *More than one God*? How could that be?

We passed by the telegraph office, a small wooden structure set back from the road behind a small yard and wedged in between two larger buildings. It appeared to be closed. The one large, square window was dark but held my gaze as we moved by, looking like still pond water with so much below and unknown.

Four or five men stood about below the narrow porch, and after I raised a hand at one fellow's wave, he called out that the agent would be back soon. "They've been up half the night," he said.

A minute later, and much to my surprise, I spotted Isis sitting alone by the iron railing near the top of the Town House steps. When had I ever seen her in Peterborough? Or at any public occasion? She caught sight of me as we approached the intersection and stood to wave hello. I returned it perfunctorily and almost at once soured at myself for withholding the keenness I too felt. We parked the wagon and went back to stand on upper Main Street; I looked all up and down for Isis but couldn't find her.

The parade was far shorter than the ones I had thrilled at as a younger boy. The band marched up Main Street with but five or six horns and three drums. Only three hay-wagon floats followed, though I heard the first drawing loud hurrahs; and as it came up I saw two fellows in the bed bobbing this way and that while jabbing hayforks at a pair of straw dummies suspended from poles. These were dressed all in gray, and kept spinning and tossing about, making it an effort to read the signs pinned to their chests. JOHNNY REB and TRAITOR. A ten-foot wide banner in bold lettering was fixed to the side of the wagon. GOD SAVE THE UNION.

Three white-haired fellows dressed in faded blue and red coats shuffled toward the end. Father gave them a proud wave, and as they passed by he reminded me that they were the Men of 1812. "They never fought their own, I'll tell ya that!" he said in a pointed reference that wasn't lost on me.

My earliest and fondest memories of Independence Day were of the old fire-wagon, *Aquarius,* which always brought up the rear. As a three or four year-old I had sat on Ned's shoulders, gazing wondrously at the lengths of brass tubing and the gleaming maze of loops—and at the merry men all around it, who, like attendants to a queen in their fire-red shirts, tossed peppermints out into the crowding, squealing, children. There were only half as many men this year, but they tossed candy.

"I guess there better not be a fire til this war runs out," said Father.

We made our way back along Grove Street toward a deep, elm-shaded lawn where folks had begun gathering to picnic. Two walkways rose diagonally from each end to meet below the bell tower of the massive, brick Phoenix Mill. On the ascent Mama stopped to speak to a friend, then again and a little longer with a second woman, who also had a son in the army.

Bread, cheese, cold pork, pickles, lemonade, watermelon and berry pie, it was all there, just as always, I ate my fill. But Mama took little, and she had spoken less, if anything, until all at once she began a steady chatter, going oddly on and on with one string of gossipy comments following another. Then she turned almost mean-spirited!

"Look," she said. "Look at Cartwright there. Is he still drinking, I thought he'd quit. By the look of him I'd have my doubts."

"All right, Lucy, that's enough now," Father said.

Mama's feverish eyes fell to a spreading knife she held in her fist and she regarded it for a few moments before setting it aside.

Some five minutes later a burst of cheering rose from down around the corner on Main Street.

In sudden recognition the entire slope stilled.

The telegraph office!

Two young fellows, waving and hollering, came racing through the intersection and halted below.

"Victory!" shouted one with both arms up thrust. I sprang to my feet. "We licked 'em!" hollered the other as he repeatedly jabbed a fist.

After we'd all calmed, I asked Mama if I could go down to the Office.

"Most certainly you may not!"

"Aw, Mama!"

"And don't you raise your voice to me, young man!"

Father leaned in. "Let him go if he's a mind. Won't be no names yet anaway."

Mama looked back at him in anguish.

Men were crowded in shoulder to shoulder in a space no larger than my bedroom. But with them all in a jabber about what the victory meant, or didn't, it wasn't hard to work my way forward to the high counter.

"Somebody send you, son?"

I straightened. "Yes, sir. I'm Sam Dascomb's son."

He took a moment. "Ah yes, the Second I believe That right?"

"Yes, sir, My brother's Lieutenant Dascomb. Company G."

"Yes, yes," the agent nodded as he went to the yellow dispatch sheets on the counter. "The Second, the Second," he murmured, thumbing pages, then he looked up. "You want to see this?" he said, with something in his voice giving me a prickle. "Son?" he said.

I pulled a breath and nodded. He turned a half sheet toward me and slid it along the counter.

VICTORY AT HAND. NEW HAMPSHIRE FIFTH AND TWELFTH SEVERELY ENGAGED; SECOND SCATTERED. MANY OFFICERS KILLED OR WOUNDED.

I seized.

I heard the man's considerate voice after I'd turned.

I dropped myself on the planks at the end of the porch to sit and stare at the brick wall three feet away. I don't know how long it was til I heard my name.

"Marty? Is something wrong?" The softness in her voice told me she already knew half of it, but I didn't stir. "What is it, Marty?"

"Nothing," I said. "Officers."

"Officers? But not ···"

I shook my head and kept staring. My heart beat. My chest rose and fell.

She sat down. I felt her hand on my shoulder.

It was a minute til I told her there hadn't been any names, then another before I began saying I didn't know what to say to Mama. Then a voice drawled in.

"Af-fter-noon folks."

Isis turned sharply, and I followed, to see the smile spread into Croslin's face as he stood regarding me.

"Marty, ain't it?" he said, but then cut away to Isis. "I been looking for you, missy." He held a parcel wrapped in twine under one arm. He was dressed in a new denim shirt. "Took me a while, too, he said. "I thought we'd agreed where to meet."

Mr. Croslin was a short, thin man with a stature made greater by a menacing presence. His eyes were small and round, and they were about all you saw, for most of his face was hidden behind a massive brown beard. In the few exchanges I'd had with him over the years, he'd left the feeling that I counted for nothing.

"I saw Marty," said Isis. "His brother's in the army."

"Well, no harm I guess," he said, tossing a grin. "Look here, I got ye something." He held out the brown packet.

Isis looked at it but said nothing.

"Well then, up to home," he said. "Anyhow, I thought ye deserved something and this here'll fit ye fur a while."

"I needed to talk to Marty," she said.

Croslin eyed me a moment. "Yer brother's down there, ain't he?"

"Yessir"

"Wa'll. Most of em'll come through all right. It's only a percent that don't."

After my shallow nods he returned to Isis.

"Anaway, Missy. We best be off."

I went back up the hill and lied, mostly. I said I'd only heard that the Second had been in the middle of it.

THREE

An evening storm brought a change in the air, which hung thick in the meetinghouse the following morning and held the scent of stale wood smoke, though the stoves hadn't been fired in weeks. And once or twice, amid all the crowding and greeting inside, I turned from the smell of strong perfume. But worst was the oppression of my woolen jacket, one of Ned's hand-downs that had once been too big but now bound me at the shoulders.

I sat wedged in beside Mama at the end of our high-sided pew, five rows back and to the right of Reverend Caswell, where a shift in the pulpit put him once again in a shaft of light from an upper window; it gleamed in his hair and lent his face a pinkish hue. He'd been speaking for the better part of an hour.

"So while we rejoice in this great triumph, at the same time we are mindful that it must come at a mighty cost." He paused. "But while we know that the darkest of shadows may fall, yet we know also that we are prepared. For we are in His hands and to Him have we committed all our hearts, all our hopes and fears." He paused. "And now, before the Almighty and with Him, let us together quiet ourselves in prayer."

I lowered my head and watched Mama's hands clasp. I put mine close but did not join them.

Throughout this morning Mama had appeared serene, and I was grateful for whence it came. But Mama's comforts were not mine and whatever abided in her was missing in me. I was unable to 'give my hopes and fears to the Lord.'

But hadn't I tried! Over and over. But never more strongly than on an April day three years before when I'd been trusted with a short ride on Old Bob in the pasture behind the barn.

So-o Bobby. You found a hole, did you?

I didn't see it, Father! I DIDN'T! I DIDN'T SEE IT!

It ain't your doin', Mart. It don't take much at his age, I shouldn't have sent him out with you.

Father went back to the house for the gun, and I sat there with Bob, leaning in over him, saying I love you's into his quiet eyes. My heart felt to bursting. And I wished it would.

I was awakened by agonized dreams for a night or two afterward, once by a throbbing at my ankle!

But how could God have allowed this to so faithful a soul as our Bob! I'm certain Father felt the loss as much as me. But he had God. And God had his ways. And Bob was with Him in a better place. Father urged me to pray for "peace of heart", and I did, but my heart remained a gaping hole. And we hadn't even been able to bury Old Bob, since our rock-filled New Hampshire soil wouldn't yield the space for him.

Reverend Caswell came around from the pulpit to look down at the eighty of us shouldered up below.

"In the words of the savior, 'blessed are they that mourn, for they shall be comforted'. And when we find that our sufferings most abound, then shall His spirit within us so much more abound."

Hymns had always been the one welcome part of the Sabbath hour. Sometimes they moved me, and at times, stirred by the organ's deep tones and the swell of voices conjoined, I felt myself in touch with something wonderful beyond. On this morning, the final hymn was one I did not much care for but knew well.

God moves in a mysterious way
His wonders to perform;
He plants his steps in the sea,
And rides upon the storm.

It was the kind of image that as a small child I had come to fear: An ancient and white-bearded stern face—and a God who might well decide what to do with *me*!

My Christian upbringing had begun early, as had my brother's before me. Both of us listened to and later were required to spend daily time with the Bible. Father questioned us. On Sunday evenings we gathered for family readings. And for the few transgressions, when Father felt compelled to take the strap to his sons, his punishment was administered only after we were given a short scriptural lesson delivered without anger and almost kindly.

By the age of nine or ten, beginning one summer after Ned returned from Dartmouth College, new questions began to arise in me,. Father had been skeptical about Ned's desire to go on to college. He had dismissed the need for education beyond reading and writing and some numbers; he said most everything you needed could be gotten from the one Book, from your parents, and if need be, from a tradesman. But he came around gradually once Ned began talking about a possible future in the ministry—though it came with a caution about Ned "turning himself into something fancy."

And so one summer evening at the dinner table, the warning seemed to bear itself out, though the incident ended amicably, rather than in the strong words that scarred several later disputes. Ned had made a remark about not accepting the literal or historical truth of some scriptures.

Nope, Father said. The whole of it was entirely truthful as written.

"But there's an example, Father, in the very first pages."

Father stopped his fork above his plate and said, "Let's hear it."

"It's when God warns Adam and Eve not to eat of the tree of knowledge, and he says, 'For if you do, you will surely die.'"

Father tipped his head back. "That's right."

"But they didn't, Father! They didn't die!"

Father's eyes widened. "Oh?" Ned puzzled a moment, then laughed. "You know what I mean. They ate of the fruit, but they did *not* die of it."

"Not right away. No," Father returned. "But they died to God's grace, and that there's what begun all the sin that come after."

"Except that's *not* what it says. That's *you* reading into it. There's no explanation. God simply says 'you will die.' That's all! That's all he says."

Father leaned in over the table. "This what's coming of yer education up there, is it? Ain't it clear more was meant? Yer sayin' there was no explanation, but it's all in what came after in human history." Father sat back. "You know this, Ned. The whole of the Old Testament ... that's all the tellin' what it means."

Ned set his knife and fork together in the center of his plate and looked up. "Why wouldn't God just say what he meant? Why make a statement, then leave the rest of it all up to us to figure out?"

Father folded his arms, narrowed his eyes. "Thin ice," he said. "That way yer on is thin ice."

Ned sat back, then smiled. "Let's think about this," he said. "Here it is *me* arguing for the literal truth, and the one that's interpreting is *you!*"

Mama stood abruptly from her chair and said, "All right, you two. I've waited my turn, and now I'll give it to you in one word." She looked at each of us in turn, slyly. "Apples!"

We three looked up, open-mouthed.

"That's right, Apples. I don't believe God forbid us those, did he." She leaned into the table on both hands. "No, He did not, and wouldn't you know, I've baked a pie full of them just this afternoon." She peered down her eyes. "Now which of you fellows will have a piece?"

· · ·

I cleaned up after milking the next day while Father went into town. I hadn't gone to school and was cutting some flowers for Mama by the front porch at midmorning when the wagon returned. From a ways off I could see that Father sat up more than usual on the bench. And when his face came clear I chilled.

I remember Father's hat cradled on the kitchen table before him and the scent of fried vegetables in the air. Father had called up the stairs, and we waited til Mama came down to sit with us. Father began quietly. He said Ned was in the fighting. I fixed my eyes on the saltshaker.

Wounded, I heard. Saturday. The whole room felt like a stilled heart.

"They're sayin' it may be severe," he said and Mama let out a groan. Father leaned in far.

"Now we don't know, Lucy. We don't know. Nothin's firm."

Later in the day we were brought the words of another dispatch. *Lt. Dascomb recovered. Chest wound. Resting in field hospital.* And still later another neighbor came by to tell us that our famed New Hampshire nurse, Harriet Dame, had been attending Ned.

· · ·

For a week, while all the world about me seemed drained of its pulse and color, we waited and heard nothing. But on a Sunday afternoon on the twelfth day of July, my father summoned us once more into the kitchen. He looked up from his folded hands on the table, then held his eyes in the space between Mama and me to tell us that Ned had died.

From beyond the window not long after came the short shrill shrieks of a jay.

FOUR

The boy is on his thighs and elbows pulling his way through grass so tall and thick it crowds out the night. The stalks are coarse and sharp-edged. His hands and forearms have been cut, his cheeks sting. He has been clawing himself along, forever, it seems. But now, inches from his nose, a narrow track, a dim, foot-wide tunnel. A rush of air, two riveted eyes, rabbit flank, frenzy of legs. Past and gone, but at once another burst. Blazing eyes, teeth like daggers, a fury of limbs. The boy shudders awake and throws himself over onto his back.

    I stared up, wide-eyed and heaving breaths for half a minute, but my stomach kept on churning after I'd settled. I got up and went down the hall to the head of the stairs, knowing what I would find. I stood and looked down into the faint amber light from the parlor below before going down to sit with Mama in the armchair. Neither of us spoke til a few minutes later when she offered to warm some milk for me in the kitchen.

· · ·

Two or three days later I experienced a wholly different, though scarcely less unearthly encounter than those of my nightmares. On a mild evening I went down and settled against Secret Rock. The river came by as always, slow and steady. I watched twigs and blades of grass drift by and after a while came to feel something of their quiet presence stolen into me.

    I caught sight of a mallard a ways upstream, a drake with its green head shining in the late day sun. It came on easily on the glossy surface, turning its head here and there slowly. Its eyes stopped on me, and as they held, I felt a sense recognition, and then more, a kind of union, as if in some elemental way we were not separate, not different, but more than anything else *the same*.

The moment felt electric but didn't last. In a sudden beat of its wings my little friend lifted away, and I watched him wheel and level off to cross the sky toward Mount Monadnock. I watched into the distance til he resolved into a speck and disappeared.

• • •

I kept at my daily chores as usual. One was splitting kindling for the cookstove, and one evening I paused with the hatchet in my hand. I glanced down at my thigh and imagined myself missing a stroke.

Father and I said very little in the barn, but I found the company of the cows comforting. Their mournful eyes were like mirrors and I felt even closer to them now. I'd never cottoned much to garden work, but now, once or twice, I went back out to search for shoots of weed to pull. But whenever I could, I went to be alone in my room, sometimes staring up from my bed for what might have been hours at a time. I didn't go to school, though one afternoon I took a book from the shelf. I held it before me for a few seconds before pitching it at the wall. I ate little, some, forcing myself. Mama forced me. We were all of us dull: the house, the farm, land, the sky. Everything felt of a piece, and so far from me and my breathing and the beating of my heart.

Then one day Father returned in the wagon, and something in his expression gave me a bolt.

This had all been wrong! A mistake!

Mama herself had voiced this. I remember a morning at the table, with Father detailing once more how the regiment had been sent forward into a peach orchard, its exposure, and how the casualties had all been counted -193 in the 2nd, as it turned out. The names all confirmed finally.

"They were with him in the hospital, Lucy. Eight or nine days, weren't it?" he said, the patience in his voice holding throughout, while Mama sat staring past his shoulder.

Every morning when I came downstairs, I found Mama, with her hair down about her shoulders and the oil lamp still burning beside her in the armchair she'd turned to face out a window. Her eyes were empty and dark-rimmed as she went about the house, enduring only the essentials of her usual work. One afternoon she set a dish of potatoes on the table, all peeled and cut, but not steaming, nor even boiled! Father looked at me, then with an affectionate smile up at Mama.

"These'll be a little hard on the jaw, Lucy, don't you think?"

Father had always been predictable in the order and execution of his daily tasks – in the village I'd once heard him compared to the hands of a clock - and almost nothing about him had changed. Every morning and again in the afternoon he recorded the weight of each cow's yield in the notebook he kept in the milk room. Two or three times during the summer months he set traps out back for the woodchucks. One afternoon he came in with one, and just as always he treated the hide and tacked it up to dry on the south wall of the barn. After walking the north pasture and the woodlot, he came in muttering about all the gray birch coming in, then I watched him go straight to one of his farm books to note something.

It took awhile before it truly began to puzzle me at seeing him almost unaffected, but one thing did shift: Father had never been a man of many words, but with Mama and me going about almost mute, he began to seem almost garrulous.

• • •

One evening I came up from the river into the kitchen, and Mama came out of the pantry at once to stand and regard me sternly.

"What is *that*?" she demanded, jabbing a forefinger at the table.

The envelope! The letter!

"How came you by this?"

I stared at the little square in disbelief, almost like it was a finger I hadn't noticed was missing.

"I found this under your bed!"

I stammered at something.

"Speak to me!" she said.

The breaks in my voice subsided after I told her I hadn't dared bring it to them, and why. Then I gave her all of it, including the unexpected impression Robert Smith had left upon me. She listened throughout and said nothing, and at the end she came around and held me.

She said she'd been dusting in my room, and I should have known she'd find it. Indeed, in the few preceding days Mama had taken to compulsive cleaning: scouring and scrubbing, mopping, beating out carpets in the yard, straightening furniture in every corner. But with one exception: Ned's room behind the blank face of his door.

She pulled out a chair for me, then sat herself at an angle beside.

"I don't know what to make of it," she wondered. He never spoke of a woman. And this is a woman's hand."

"What *did* he say about being down there?" I said and repeated that the Negro wouldn't tell me anything.

"A mother does want to know these things," Mama sighed.

"There ain't nothing to do with it anyway," I said.

"Well, you were a good brother," she said with a cloud in her eye. "You addressed it." She drew a long breath. "We'll leave it in his desk," she said and rose, and took a step or two away before stopping. She set fists at her hips, but only for only a second or two before turning abruptly to hasten off into the parlor - and return with the letter opener!

"I guess we'll just see about this," she said.

She opened a once-folded, pale blue sheet, and I watched as she read, as she raised her eyes to look past me for a few moments, then return and take more time with it. I saw her face soften and turn sad. She set the note paper down gently, as if it were fragile, and turned her back to me.

"Mama. Mama," I said quietly.

She reached a hand behind and pointed at the table.

14 June, 1863
Dear Ned,

I am sending this letter with Robert. I don't suppose you know that he escaped to Canada in the year before the war, He is now coming south to join the Union Army, where I am all but certain you must be yourself.

I thought I should never trouble you. I came to Montreal some time ago myself after life became unbearable for all people of color, especially I must tell you now, for a young woman with a child.

Yes, Ned. Sophie is nearly three years old now, and sometimes when she smiles, I see you in her face.

Please be assured that I have nothing to ask of you, as both Sophie and I are in better circumstances than we could ever have hoped for. I have only concluded that at long last you should know of one who carries you on.

I hope you are well, and I wish you to know that you are never forgotten.
With my fondest regards,
Marie Desdunes

. . .

Sometime during the night a hard rain woke me from a dream. A letter had come from Ned saying he was trapped in a school, and to come get him. I was on a road driving at the wagon, but getting nowhere. Wheels up to the axles in mud. Men laughing, standing by.

It was a fitful sleep, but by morning I had myself convinced that it was all lies, that these people only wanted something from Ned. Even Robert Smith! How he had fooled me! Father had been right all along about niggers, and if it weren't for them there wouldn't be no war and Ned ...

Resentment bloomed in me like a dark flower, and though I hadn't slept well, I went downstairs with energy and a sense of purpose, which I voiced to Father as we walked out to the barn.

"That letter, "I said. "That don't sound like a colored woman to me."

"It don't matter much now," he said.

"But it ain't true!"

Father kept on, and by the barn entry I tried again. "It's all made up, Father! All lies!"

I had my anger now, and anger would keep me going: anger at these people and their letter; anger at Ned for leaving me; anger at his notions about slave freedom and saving the Union. At God and my father. At myself.

Father turned and fixed me sternly.

"What's in there, Martin, it ain't made up; there ain't no reason for it. "

Yet another shock came two days later when Father bade me sit with him on the porch steps after dinner. He told me that a "judgment had been rendered" upon Ned. He had believed in Negroes as equals, then gone to teaching them and taken up with one. Father said that Ned's fate was of his own making, the consequences of his sins. And then came this.

"I've told your mother, Mart, that after today I intend to speak no more of your brother." He sat for just a few moments before rising to start for the barn.

My head had gone thick, and I don't know what I did or what I felt for the next hour before I found myself in the parlor entry before Mama. She was sitting at the far end and said she'd been waiting; she beckoned me to come sit.

She said it was hard for all of us but she wanted me to know she didn't share Father's thinking. She said she was hopeful that with time he'd change his mind. "But for the time being …"

"But what do *you* think, Mama?" I interrupted. "What do *you* think about Ned!"

She stiffened. "Nothing changes! Nothing! Ned will *always* be my son and I've said that to your father."

"But it's not true! That woman! None of it's true!"

She gave me a thin, sad smile and said, "Maybe one day we'll see. Maybe one day we'll find out more."

A few days later Father brought in an envelope bearing a Pennsylvania postmark and the printed blue lettering of the Second New Hampshire Volunteers.

3rd Corps Hospital
July 14, 1863
Mr. Dascomb,
It is with feelings of grief of no ordinary kind that I find myself compelled to write to you the sad tidings of the passing of your son. He was wounded on the second day of July while engaged on the left flank of our lines. He was shot beneath his sword arm, the ball passing through the left lung and lodging beyond. He was kept on the field for three days and nights in the Rebel lines when he was brought back by our men on the fifth. He died on the twelfth at twenty minutes past twelve. He is buried in a beautiful spot near the 3rd Corps Hospital under an apple tree. The Hon. Fred Smith has a sketch of the grave which he intends to have lithographed. As soon as I get back to the regiment I shall take an inventory of his effects and have the same forwarded to you. Let me also take this opportunity to say that your son's virtues were as great as his heroic bravery and courage were undaunted.

Hoping that you may receive the consolations from above which a wise Providence in his mercy bequeaths to the mourner, I remain yours truly,

James H. Platt
Capt. Co. G 2nd Reg. N.H.V.

Father had no objection when Mama expressed a desire to send it along to the *Peterborough Transcript* to be made public.

I went back to the letter several times in the next day or two and found it restoring me some. It seemed to affect Mama, too—or something did. One afternoon as I reached the top of the stairs on the way to my room, I halted at hearing her down the hall in her room. Humming! It was an old familiar tune, a lullaby!

Too-raloo-raloora; too-raloo-ralay

. . .

Visions haunted my sleep: a woman with no expression looking at me in silence; the face and eyes of my favorite cow, Genevieve, though she'd been gone for several years; the face of Scoonie Fenn in close, shouting into my face and spitting past my ear.

I hadn't been to school or off the farm at all in a fortnight, but one evening after dinner Mama suggested I go along into town and seek out a friend by the green.

"Take the bag of marbles," she said. "It'll do you good."

Marbles?

"Marbles?" I said.

"Listen here! You go on now or I'll find something you'll like a whole lot less."

I said the they were in Ned's room, but to my surprise she told me to go up. She said she'd been in there herself.

It felt strange, seeing everything still as it was: the checked blue-and-yellow wallpaper, the same frayed quilt on the bed all drawn up as if waiting for a return; his bureau and desk with the oak-framed diploma above. And the shelf of books.

I went over and ran my eyes along the leather spines. Augustine, Aquinas, Bunyan, Milton, Pope, Thoreau, Emerson.

Emerson! I recalled the conflict one night when Ned had come back after attending one of his lectures. Father had begun it by saying the man was "full of ten-cent stuffery."

Essays: Second Series. R.W. Emerson

I turned through a few pages, a few with notes penciled in the margins. He had drawn a bold star above one short verse, and underscored several lines, and as I read it through I saw some reflection of my brother.

A moody child and wildly wise
Pursued the game with joyful eyes
Which chose, like meteors, their way
And rived the dark with private ray:
They overleapt the horizon's edge,
Searched with Apollo's privilege;
Through man, and woman, and sea, and star
Saw the dance of nature forward far;
Through worlds, and races, and terms, and times
Saw musical order, and pairing rhymes.

I imagined what Father would say if he saw this.
Turkey Feathers!
I returned the book to its place and went to the bottom drawer for the marbles.

FIVE

I looked about at the head of the village green, and eased, seeing but a few people and no one of my age or acquaintance. The long green ahead was vacant. Two women stood chatting out front of Mr. Wilson's store on the left. Before the blacksmith's shop further along, a group of men at a game of cards sat on stools around a small round table. Along the Francestown Road to the right behind picket fences and well-tended yards. a row of brick and clapboard houses looked out onto the common My eye lingered on a fellow and his wife taking in a pleasant evening in rocking-chairs on their front porch. Out that way, too, I heard the glee of several children at play.

I turned to see no one in the churchyard just to my right. I went in to my pocket and rubbed fingers about the bag of marbles and thought about going around back by the horse sheds to shoot Chase with myself. I squinted to read a sign on the church lawn.

BEAN SUPPER. 6 P.M. SATURDAY
Didn't they KNOW! How were they going on with these?

When I looked down the common again, a movement beyond the base of a tree half way along caught my eye. A bare foot. And then a shift that sent a thrill through me when I glimpsed a length of her washed-out gown. I lurched forward, then halted to cup my hands.

"Ise!" My voice was hoarse. She didn't move and I took a few steps in to call out more loudly.

She came scrambling up and whirled, and stood, staring, then she broke and came rushing up at me and if I hadn't braced, she'd have pitched me over. She pinned my arms and gripped hard and long and when she let go and backed away, we just stood looking at one another.

She told me she'd come in to the green nearly every day. I looked down.

"I didn't know if you ever would," she said.

I said I hadn't done much and again we stood, til finally I told her I'd brought some marbles.

Out behind the church I took Ned's favorite orange and brown-striped shooter; she chose a smaller one, with blue and cream-colored swirls. We took turns at Chase and spoke hardly at all; but once, when I snapped from only inches away and missed, she let out a squeal she cut off at once, saying she didn't mean it.

It was fifteen minutes til we felt safe or settled enough to face the heavy presence that hung like some dark ghost between us; and perhaps she knew it would be hers to broach. She straightened herself before me and asked if they were sending Ned home. I said, no, that he'd been buried by the battlefield. I told her about the tree and the ceremony. And the lithograph engraving.

"What's that?" she said. I told her, then I told her about the letter we'd got from the captain. She looked down, and it was done. All we both wanted or needed for the moment.

I asked if she'd been to school.

She frowned. "Just once," she said. I asked why. "Nothing. I just didn't go back," she said and turned and lobbed her marble.

I asked if something happened, but she started away. "You don't want to hear," she said and shook her head when I said I did.

She knelt and took aim. My ball was a good three or four away, but she struck it full on. Then she stood and beckoned me off to sit on the back steps of the church.

She'd tell me what happened, she said, but first she wanted to know how far it was to Keene. I guessed it was twenty miles, then asked why.

"Nothing much," she said, "but I ain't going back to school as long as that woman's there."

She told me that a week ago Alf had brought in a frog and put it in the water bucket. A few of the boys knew about it, but not little Nellie, who went over for a drink and let out a shriek.

"You know what that woman done!" she said with a face turned fierce. "She went over to that pail and just like that she snatched the poor thing up."

"Jeee-eez!"

"She did! Then she went over and held … she held it down on the table and took out a hairpin!"

"NO-OOH?"

"She did! And I ran out! First I hollered at her, then I ran out. And some boys did, too. Two of them and we none us went back."

But that wasn't the end of it. She sat still, staring off, and when she spoke a minute later it was a struggle to hear at first.

"··· what he done?" she breathed into the air in disbelief.

"Who?" I said.

"Him!" she barked and at once I knew who she meant. "I told him about it up to home and he only laughed." She turned. "He just laughed at it!"

I had drawn my head back and could only look back at her, open-mouthed.

She sat up. "Hey, I been keeping this. I got some peppermint." She went to the pocket in her gown, saying she'd found a penny and gone into Wilson's. Then she said she had remembered the few times we'd found Ned in town and he'd always gotten us mints. A thin smile had emerged at her thoughts of Ned, and from that, perhaps, I found myself able to take up.

"Hey!" I said "Remember that time with the snake! I guess he thought that was something, all right."

"You did, at least!"

"No, no! Him!"

We had come out of the store, the three of us, and were standing around savoring the first mint when Ned spotted it, said it was as fat an old cuss as ever he'd seen. It was at least three feet long and had large reddish-brown splotches all down its back; but it didn't move as we approached and stood over it. I said I thought it was dead, but Isis shook her head. She said it just an old fellow that had too much sun. She went to one knee, and as her hands slid under, the 'old fellow' could muster only the slightest response. It hung heavy and limp over her forearms when she brought it up.

Ned and I stood by agape as she walked off, stopping once to turn and give us an earnest glance before continuing out back, where she stooped to set it down in some thick growth.

"Don't that beat all," said Ned. "There ain't two folks in this town would do that. Or could!"

I asked her if she wasn't scared back then. She smiled and said no, she guessed it was only people to be afraid of. She brought out two more mints. She told me she used to wish Ned had been her brother, too, and reminded me of the time at the Witness Tree when she'd climbed too high and Ned had to come out for her.

But at that the pain came up in me. I choked and pulled my head away.

"Oh, Marty! I'm sorry, I'm so so sorry."

I shook my head hard. I sprang up and rushed away.

"I'll come in tomorrow," she called after. "Okay? Okay?"

I kicked at stones in the road for a time, then broke into a run and raced myself out of breath, til not far from home I dropped into the chickweed beside the road.

A few minutes later I went on, but then, at sight of the Witness Tree ahead on the crest, silhouetted against the deepening sky, I halted.

It had been two years ago when three of us boys had dared her, kept pushing her to go up as high as she could. It wasn't like Isis to care, but eventually she gave in to our doubts, our taunts. The old beech was seventy feet tall, at least four feet wide, and scarred by dozens of initials, including my own—and one could still see faint remains of the diagonal markings that identified it as a boundary "witness." She had made it halfway to the top, but only to get stuck after misjudging what it took to come back down. She made a few cautious attempts before it was clear she couldn't manage it. At first, we laughed. Then we got nervous and looked at each other, beginning to panic.

I yelled something up and then bolted for the house. I found Father, and Father said he'd better get Ned and I ran back to shout up word of help coming and after a while the two of them came sauntering up the rise, with Ned carrying a coil of heavy rope over his shoulder. I remember him looking up at Isis and the grin he broke that relieved us all at once.

"Hey there, young lady!" he hollered up "You been showin' these boys up again have ya?" He turned and held a flat hand over his brow, then playing it up further, he bent exaggeratedly out toward the east and pointed. "Now, young lady," he called out. "Take a gander out that way, will ya. and give us a count of the ships in Boston Harbor!"

Five minutes later he had made his way up enough to lob the rope over a branch she could reach.

And afterward we all went back to the house, where Mama gave us some stern words before sitting us around the kitchen table for lemonade.

SIX

July passed into August, and while Mama continued to encourage but didn't press me to return to school, I did manage to take up where I'd left off with *Oliver Twist*.

I had been in to see Isis twice again, and at the last she'd confided that she was thinking of leaving home, of running away. To California of all places! She wouldn't tell why, and even snapped when persisted, but I knew it could only be one thing. And I didn't really believe her, even when she said she had a ten dollar gold-piece her mother had once given her. I thought that at most she might try some small thing and then realize how impossible it was. Still, I thought of her a lot, and I came to feel that our two afflictions made us almost like kin. I imagined her waking up of a morning and going about in a darkened world of her own up there on Butternut Mountain.

No more had been spoken about the letter or the woman and child, at least not in my presence. But I came to notice a softening in Mama's face, and one day I saw her go about from one task to another with a preoccupied air and a mellowed expression, almost a smile. I was curious but loath to disturb it with a question.

Nor had we three together spoken of Ned, even if it felt sometimes as if he were there among us. Meals were punctuated with periods of solemn silence, and sometimes Father excused himself early to go out to work he had begun at restoring a carriage that had sat for two decades in a far corner of the hayloft. Only once had I gone in to lift under the oilcloth to see the railings turned to rust and the gold trim all dulled. I'd been told, that Grampa Dascomb had had a failure of his heart while sitting in this buggy one day at the end of a ride. He had died right there, sitting in it, and after the funeral Father had dedicated the old wagon its own space. I puzzled at his intentions in working on it so.

∙ ∙ ∙

On the way in with the egg basket one morning, a butterfly of a kind I'd never seen crossed my path. It was all glossy black but with a white blaze through each wing. I stopped to watch it by, and on. Floating, beating its wings, then drifting again; on and on til it resolved into the orchard below the house. I thought of my mallard at the river and it seemed so long ago.

∙ ∙ ∙

One day Father told me that the second cut of hay—the rowen, as it is called— was coming in earlier than usual. I knew, of course, that he would sorely need me. It normally took three days and the effort of at least two grown men to get the grass down, spread, turned, dried, and finally pitched into the wagon to be taken to the loft. But the matter became more troublesome when Father discovered that his only grown-up help was still away. Jim Henry had gone off to Fitchburg, as he did every now and then— where it was common knowledge he drank whiskey with his cousins. Everyone knew Jim as a simpleminded man, but he was a steady worker when you had him, and with hired men scarce during the war, Father depended on him more than he liked. Now it would be only the two of us at perhaps the most important of our summer tasks. Six weeks earlier I had been of modest help, but even a June sun had wilted me badly enough on an afternoon to have Father send me to the house.

That evening I stood by watching Father peen the blades, and despite my mild protests, he insisted on measuring me up again to make sure I "hadn't changed any". My scythe had been Ned's for years, but Father always checked to see that the grips were adjusted just so. And he had me practice yet again. And hadn't I heard *this* before!

"When you start git'n tired, see you think to keep the heel down. And keep yer turn nice and easy."

At a quarter after four the next morning Father and I came out of the house to fill the jugs at the pump. I looked up and to my great surprise and relief, there stood Jim Henry! Out by the road in the starlight in his high-waisted overalls, his scythe clasped in both hands before him.

He grinned at my hail and in a raspy voice called back, "Guess I ain't late, am I?"

"Right on time, Jim!" said Father, suddenly aglow. "Yer right on time."

Jim was well into his thirties, but still far more of a boy than a man. He was of medium height, stalk thin, and his long, narrow face reminded me of a hatchet blade, even if the notion was entirely out of keeping with his temperament. As a young boy he had been kicked by a cow, taking most of the blow at his shoulder, but some at the head. But if his mind had been affected, his heart remained full, and I'd heard Mama say that she knew a few men who'd have done better with a "thump on the head" like the one he'd taken.

As we set off, Father inquired after Jim's mother and father, with whom he still lived. He had Jim promise to send his regards, then pronounced the weather just about right for "a good day in the field." His mood was as high as I'd seen it in weeks.

We paused to survey the north meadow that stretched out before us between the road and the river that bordered it below. It was a full two-acres of timothy and ryegrass, but in the murky light it made me think of a body of still water. Father turned to us with a smile and said he had a question: Did we boys know why it was the grass laid down best before the sun got up full? The answer would give one of us first crack at the switchel jug later on.

I had no idea, and I could see Jim puzzling - before his face brightened.

"Cuz it ain't hot!" he said emphatically.

"Now that might be it some of it," said Father, thumbing at his chin. "But there's more."

"Don't know," Jim said. "Don't know that."

Father looked at me. I shrugged.

"All right, then. When the grass is still wet it, don't bend away so much and yer blade'll come through easier."

Jim gave a little hop, then a clap at his thigh. "Ain't that a fact!" he exclaimed, then blushed proudly when Father told him he was glad to see him thinking so much.

Then came another query: How many strokes would it take us to lay all this down?

"Ten thousand!" I said.

"Close," Father said, beaming. "Ten thousand in each acre."

And so we began. Father stepped off first, then Jim, after spitting into his hands and rubbing them together. I waited another beat or two.

"No waste, now," Father called back. "See that you cut low!"

I'd heard this, put one way or another, most every one of my days out here: how a good mower never left the thickest part of the stalk in the ground; how 'an inch at the bottom was as good as two at the top.'

And before the end of this long day, the three of us would be in and out and back three times - or was it four! The aim was to get as much down and spread as we could in the morning; after lunch we'd rake it into windrows to dry. After supper we'd return yet again to bring it all up into haycocks.

For two hours we mowed, then broke to go back for the morning milking and breakfast. Jim and I kept up a brisk pace behind Father. And then it dawned on me that Jim hadn't spoken of Ned! I wondered if was for lack of proper words, or did he just not know. But as we approached the barn, Jim took a quick step forward.

"Mister Dascomb?" he said a little timidly.

"What's that, Jim?" said Father over his shoulder. We went on a pace or two. "What is it, Jim?" he said.

"I heard somethin' bad," said Jim.

Our footsteps returned noisily for several seconds.

"What you heard, Jim. I'm afraid it's true."

More footsteps.

"I heard ⋯" said Jim, cautiously.

One or two footfalls.

"Yes. That's right, Jim," said Father.

The barn and house were in sight now.

"Mister Dascomb. I ain't so good saying things."

"Don't you worry none, Jim. You don't need no words."

"But Missis Dascomb," said Jim, pleading.

"It's all right. She'll understand. Don't you fret."

Jim's voice pitched up in despair. "It jus don't feel good," he said. And then, "Mr. Dascomb. I got to!"

Father stopped and turned to him. "And that'll be fine if you do, Jim. You just say what you want."

Jim looked at me, then back at Father and raised his chin proudly. "Ned Dascomb weren't never but kindly to me," he said. "Never, and that's a fact!"

When we were all in the kitchen, Jim went over at once to the stove where he had some quiet words with Mama, then he returned to wait behind me at the wash stand.

But all at once he turned back to Mama.

"Miz Dascomb. Ned ain't all the way gone when I can remember him," he said.

Mama lowered her eyes into the sudden stillness.

"Thank you, Jim," she said quietly.

SEVEN

We were four hot days getting the hay in, each of them leaving me wholly reduced by the time I finally found my bed. But they also brought blessings of sorts. I slept deeply and uninterrupted, even while every morning's work began in a state that allowed me to lapse into an almost mindless rhythm.

On the fifth day I slept in to nearly noon and came down to find that Father had been in to town and returned with a letter from Frank Fletcher; and it struck me at once that it would be Frank, if anyone, who knew of a woman in Ned's life. He was my brother's oldest and closest friend. The two of them had signed into the regiment on the same day and been tent mates the last two years. He had been given a furlough and was on his way home, bringing with him what remained of Ned's belongings.

A few afternoons later Mama went about the kitchen making lemonade and ginger shortbread ahead of Frank's three o'clock arrival. I had not asked if Father would come in to sit with us, but since she'd said nothing of it, I assumed the worst. Then, before she went upstairs to change into the better of her two mourning dresses, she sat me down to tell me what she intended to say about Father's "present state of mind."

I had heard it before: that Father was suffering, too; that he felt partly responsible for all that had happened, having failed his duty with Ned; and that he considered God's judgment to have fallen on he himself as well.

I stood up and glared aside. Did she think I didn't understand! *Was I stupid?*

She apologized. She said she didn't want to make this worse for me,. But she had, and these last, syrupy words only sickened me further. I struggled to keep myself from running off.

Mama rose and said she'd be upstairs a few minutes, and I could take the tray into the parlor if I wanted.

I went down the hall and paused in the entry. Much of my time in this, the largest room in our modest home, had been spent at my father's joyless weekly readings by the heavy oak table in the corner. To me it was a somber room, and I stood wishing we could meet with Frank in the kitchen instead. And yet again I wondered how it was possible for Father to have lost his love for Ned. And if he had, *if he had*, how would it turn out for one who was even less deserving!

Out beyond the window the leaves in the lilac bush still glistened from an earlier shower.

I went outside to watch for Frank, with whom I'd had an easy, almost brotherly relationship for years. He had spent many hours at our home, many a lunch or evening meal. I wondered again if he'd know about a woman in Ned's life.

But when had the hope begun to rise that the woman might be real? And why? I didn't know, but when my stomach tightened at thought of Mama then, as I waited for Frank, the shift in me broke into awareness.

The wait wasn't long. A buckboard swung into the bend, and at sight of the kepi and blue soldier's coat, I clamored down the steps and hastened out toward the road. Frank raised an arm and hailed.

He gave me a hard clasp, then held me out at arm's length. "Hey, what's this! You're up three or four inches. 'Bout ready to top me, I'd say."

Frank was a whole head shorter than Ned, and squarely built, which made for quite a contrast with the two of them side-to-side. He had grown a mustache, though it didn't strike me as especially becoming. He looked up beyond as Mama came bustling down the porch steps to come on at a rush and take Frank in an almost fierce embrace. Both their eyes were full when they separated. But Mama brightened.

"Why Frank, you've grown a mustache!" she said and Frank blushed when she told him it looked becoming.

In the sitting room we heard about Frank's family, his mother and father and sisters. And then, yes, we *had* had quite the early summer of rain and only just now brought in the second haying. It was five minutes before Mama sat forward and asked how Frank had managed the furlough. Wasn't it unusual? Frank began with how, after Gettysburg, some higher-up had taken pity on the regiment and sent them to Maryland.

"We were on guard duty at a prison by the shore," he said, "and a number of us had some bad shellfish. I thought I was recovering pretty well, but I didn't fight it when they give me the chance to come home."

The kitchen door opened.

"That must be Sam," Mama said and greeted him when he appeared in the threshold. "Yer right on time, Come in, we've got lemonade and Frank's favorite cake."

Father went to Frank to shake hands and thank him for coming. Then he stood solemnly back and said, "But I shan't stay."

Frank shifted uneasily but didn't say anything.

"I been sore heavy, Frank, same as us all."

"Yes, sir." Frank said.

"Lucy knows it bettr'n any."

"I do," Mama said softly. "Yes."

Father asked Frank to forgive him. He said it wasn't the best time for him just now, Then he paused for a second.

"But I did come in for something, if I may," he said. "The Governor wrote about the burial being under an apple tree. Is that so?"

Yes sir, it was. And a right full ceremony, too; I can attest to it."

"Under an apple tree, you're certain of that?"

"Yes, sir, and you'd have been proud; they chose it out special."

"Shall we hear of it, Sam?" Mama said. Her face looked pinched. "Let's do, shall we!"

Father eyes had closed, and now he opened them and stepped forward to offer his hand again. He wished Frank well, then looked briefly to Mama and turned away.

The kitchen door opened and closed. Mama apologized and Frank said there was no need of it. He thought he understood.

Mama said we'd all just been in a state. She rose to come round and fill our glasses and in her seat again, she tried to get beyond.

"When I think of apple trees, Frank," she said a little wistfully, "and this peach orchard we've heard of ⋯ don't it seem like an odd place for all those terrible things?"

Frank agreed and said there were a lot of places like that in this war. Then he reached down for Ned's haversack. He said it was as good a time as any to pass it along, which he did to me alongside. Its tarred canvas sides were well worn and cracked in places. Its brass buckle was missing and looked to have been freshly torn from the closing flap. Frank said there wouldn't be as much in it as we might like.

"Them graybacks went into it before we got back out," he said. "They take whatever they can use, you know, shirts and the like. Even combs. And toothbrushes." He said they'd looked for his sword. "I dearly hoped . . . but of course they got that, too."

Then he brightened. "But his notebooks are there! They had no use for *those*!" he said with a grin.

The notebooks! Would there be ···! I tried to quell the surge in my chest.

Ned scarcely went anywhere without a pressed-board covered writing tablet, and forever at his poems and impressions of one thing and another, when one was filled, he pulled a new one from his desk. I worked my fingers about and thought I felt two. Two books and whole lot of pages!

Mama had begun to ask about the fight. "Whatever you can tell us, Frank," she was saying. "We've agreed to hear as much as you want."

And here then, was the story of the Second New Hampshire at Gettysburg.

They had camped in Maryland the night of July second, already knowing that the fighting had begun not far ahead. At two in the morning they were roused and marched double time over the border into Pennsylvania, and at about seven they fell out on a hillside. They waited and waited, for hours, Frank said. They were only a mile or two south of Gettysburg, but it wasn't til the afternoon that they were called up. Then, along with two other units and a battery, they were sent out forward of the lines to occupy a low rise in the middle of an expanse of open farmland. That was the peach orchard, he said.

"It was all rowed out with young trees. Must have been fifty of 'em, but didn't we wonder what we were doing so far out beyond the main line." He paused, as if at wonder once again. "Well, sure enough," he said, "we did hear afterward how they allowed it was a mistake."

He took a long drink, then looked across at the mantel. "Then the guns opened up," he said. "First theirs acros't, and then ours behind and then it was just shells comin' by overhead. Back and forth and on and on for a couple hours!" Frank held his eyes on the clock on the mantel. "Two hours it was," he went on, "and it weren't no use trying to talk or even shout with all them shells bursting. We just kept to the ground under those poor trees." Frank looked to be seeing it all again in wonder. Then his face tightened. "But I'll tell ya. Didn't we get ourselves all worked up. Like a nest of hornets, we were. Just wanting to *do* something!

I stole a glance at Mama. Her hands were folded easily in her lap and she held a placid look, as if she were in church.

"It went quiet then," Frank continued, "and when we sat up, what do we see but them graybacks coming out of the woods out there - and indeed, Frank was seeing it 'out there'! - Must have been a half mile of them, getting up into their ranks maybe hundred yards off." He paused for a sip and then with a narrowed eye, caught mine for second. "But that weren't all," he said. "Out south of us *another* line of 'em come out!"

"Oh, Frank!" Mama said.

I didn't think of it then, of course, but I recall now the letter Ned had once sent to *The Transcript* telling what it was like in a battle. He'd said it wasn't what you expected, and that you'd get yourself worked up to such a fury that the best parts of you got lost altogether. Then later, he said it was possible you'd find yourself kneeling with your canteen by some fellow you'd been desperate to kill only an hour before.

"There weren't nothing we could do," Frank said. He drew a deep breath and sat back, and it was a few moments til Mama spoke.

"Were you with him, Frank?" she asked quietly, and returning slight nods, Frank lowered his head. Ned had picked up a musket, he murmured. "He had to," he said.

Mama helped him. "Was it like they said?" she asked. "Just the one ball?"

Frank's head nodded. "I knelt by him," he said. "But I couldn't stay. They were nearly on us by then."

From across the room the clock ticks sounded like little voices from afar.

"Did he know it was you?"

Frank raised his head and his face warmed toward a small smile. His eyes were large and wet.

"He looked up at me," he said. "He looked up at me, Mrs. Dascomb ⋯ and he give me one of those grins!"

"Oh Frank," Mama said. "There ain't … I can't ... Oh Frank, thank you! I'm so pleased to hear that!"

Frank turned and sat himself straight at Mama.

"How it felt!" he said with his face opening wide. "What I felt then!" he repeated. "Mrs. Dascomb, in his eyes he was telling me it would be all right.

*He was tell*ing *me!*" Mama's face flushed full. "I gripped his hand for a time," Frank said, but we couldn't stay."

He went on to tell us that the Rebels abandoned the field two mornings later, and that soon after Ned was recovered from a farmhouse, where the Confederates had brought some of the wounded. He said that their nurse, Harriet Dame, had indeed cared for Ned at the south hospital, where he, too, stayed by him as much as he could. He said Ned wasn't able to converse and had mostly slept.

It was only here, I think, at the end of Frank's account that I truly accepted that Ned was no more, and as we rose a few minutes later I felt myself oddly lighter.

Mama asked if she could spend a few minutes alone with Frank, and I went out to wait below the porch. My hopes for something about the woman returned, and at length Frank came out.

But when we were alone by his wagon, he beat me to the moment by asking if I wanted to go squirreling some morning. We agreed on a day, and then I blurted it out: Had Ned had ever talked about a girl, a woman? He drew back in surprise.

"A woman from New Orleans!" I pressed. "Did he say anything about that?

He was perplexed. "No. he never said nothing, I'm afraid.

I sagged.

"Hey! Hey, what's all this, tell me."

I went on and on and Frank tried his best. He said he didn't know what to make of it, but he'd think it over. He put a hand out to my shoulder.

"Ned was never much for ..." Then suddenly he drew up, pulling his hand away. His face opened wide.

"Hold on! Hold on now. There's a poem in there don't you know!"

I scarcely heard the rest. He'd said it had surprised him, that it was there in a nice clean sheet in one of his books.

I took the porch steps at a bound and paused at the door to settle myself. Mama wasn't in the kitchen, but the haversack lay on the table where I'd left it. I waited til Mama came in from the parlor, solemnly, with her lips pressed tight. She looked spent, but I gave it no mind and pointed and asked if I could have a look at the notebooks. "If you want to," she said, and passed on toward the sink.

I went through the first notebook, found nothing and set it aside. But in the second, right under the cover and folded precisely in half, was a sheet of Ned's pale blue stationery. His hand was as careful as ever I'd seen it!

SWEET REMEMBRANCE
'Tis sweet to remember the friend that is true,
The days that were ours, too short and too few.
A voice on the breeze, a hand at the door,
That toss of your brow—forevermore.

'Tis sweet to remember, and who hast forgot,
What was lost, and we found, on the one wondrous spot.
How dear a token, and treasure of love,
Every word that was spoken ere departing above.

Must we rue our days of temptation and sin,
When fever o'ertook the temples within?
Oh, ever, forever, as long as I live,
What I never forget, I yet can forgive.

Thus always remembered, sweet light, sweet life,
Wherever I wander, in toil or in strife,
Midst every journey my spirit may know,
Here on this road—and wherever I go.

I read it through once and with hands still shaking started in a second time, but broke off.

"Mama, it's true! It's all in here!"

EIGHT

I watched her as she read and saw no reaction, no change in her face. and after a minute or two she set the page down and said she'd better start with dinner. Whatever she felt then, I decided it best not to ask. I went upstairs to spend an hour at Ned's desk with a stack of his old notebooks, hoping there might be more, something about New Orleans, a name or an address. But among the sketches, the drafts of letters, I found nothing. I read through a number of his poems. Some were grimly serious, others humorous, and I've thought for a few moments before deciding to include one of them here, something representative of my brother's lighter side, though it ends with a bitter irony. I have it before me from the folder of clippings Mama kept from the *Peterborough Transcript*.

> *THE BALLAD OF THE GUNBOAT SHOES*
> *You ask for a relic, whatever I choose,*
> *I therefore have sent you an old pair of shoes.*
> *Not having a tongue they cannot speak,*
> *Not even like new ones by making a squeak.*
>
> *But if they could speak, methinks they would tell,*
> *Some after this fashion of what them befell,*
> *In a somewhat long and eventful career,*
> *Extending quite through five months of the year.*

It carries on like this for eight or nine more stanzas, with its conclusion seeming so casual and acceptant.

A curious relic, you may think, my friend;
Perhaps a better one, soon I may send.
But if you are pleased with the tale these bear,
Then preserve and keep them with honest care.

If not, let them go the way of all trash,
The way they should go, straight to smash;
But believe me ever your soldier friend,
Till age or bullets do bring me my end.

• • •

On my fifth or sixth birthday, I had been allowed to venture into the cowbarn on my own for the first time, and I soon came to spend nearly as much time in it as in the house itself. All was communal there, though it centered in the animals far more than in we two or three humans. From my earliest carefree hours I had felt a part of that community—among the working men, the milkers and their calves, the heifers, the cats - and for half the year the flies we continually fanned away. The stirrings and soft sounds of the herd, their pungent aromas - all this surrounded and held me as if in the quiet comfort of a symphonic movement.

The barn had been built by my father's father. It was sixty feet long and thirty wide and was set some four feet below ground level to preserve a measure of heat in the winter - as well as a little respite from it in the warmer months. We kept Holsteins, but also, for the quality of their butter and buttermilk, two or three expensive, fawn-colored Alderneys. All were held in wooden stanchions in rows facing the two side walls, each holding seven or eight good-sized windows. A ten-foot-wide walkway down the middle gave ample entrance and exit for every purpose. At the far end stood a pair of high, heavy doors that opened onto an earthen slope that led up into the pastures beyond.

But for my story, perhaps the most important aspect of the barn is above, in the hayloft. To the right of the four or five stone steps leading up to the front entry and the milkroom are two calf pens and a bin for grain storage; and crowded in beyond these, as if an afterthought in construction, is a dark, narrow, plank-enclosed flight of wooden steps that pitches steeply upward.

One day Father and I readied for the afternoon milking. A week had passed since Frank's visit. Father had seemed more somber than ever, and around me, as he kept an often grim face, I sometimes wondered if this was his way of saying he wanted me to think about Ned's 'fate". Or the example of his 'sin'. Or was it only my imagining?

It was common to speak to cows at milking, especially at the approach and in coaxing them to their duty. Sometimes I sang softly to my favorites, sometimes with tunes and lyrics of my own creation. And now and then, too, I'd hear Father at some ditty - "The Blue Tail Fly" or the like - though I had heard nothing for a quite a while.

"So-o, Brindle," I said to the first of my charges as I drew the stool in close (we'd given three or four of the cows names; this one was called Dark Brindle). I stroked her swollen belly, then leaned in below to brush the udder and whisk her teats. I brought the bucket under and began the pull pause and squeeze, pull and squeeze, pull and squeeze, over and over. The milk jets hissed, the bucket began to fill, and shortly—and always to me—the barn cats chased up. The youngest always pushed in first to sit up on her hind legs and plead with cheepy cries. I gave her a burst, then shooed her off for the other two.

Brindle was one of our best, never giving less than eight quarts, and with the heavy pail, I paused for a second in the center aisle before starting for the milk room. It was a cautionary practice Father had insisted I adopt a year or two earlier when I'd been trusted to begin carrying my own pails to the cooling tub. Father's habits, his little tricks ... I had to admit their efficacy - and every now and then, when he saw me following one, it drew a compliment.

It began to rain midway through our work, then came down in torrents for a while beyond the open windows. But it had settled into an drizzle when I returned from a trip to the milkroom. Father stood in the aisle holding the stool by his side. Waiting. I saw something in his face.

"I thought I'd have a few words with you," he said as I approached. He sat himself and said he'd only take a minute. I tightened. "I went in forenoon to see Reverend Caswell," he said. "Your mother convinced me of it, and I guess it's right she did." I wanted to look away but held my eyes at his hairline. "Anaway, Mister Caswell made the case of it that it weren't mine to judge and so ... I'm going to try at that," he said.

53

It felt as if there was a kind of screen between us, and as if I knew but didn't know, and what came out then, was a term I hadn't used in years since I was little.

"Papa?" I said.

He looked off and took a few moments.

"Ned's a good deal to answer for," he said firmly, "but I guess it ain't to any of us here."

I felt my knees gone soft.

He turned and with an effort heaved himself up.

"That's the whole of it," he said, looking down at me. He smiled. "Now, those ladies been waitin' long enough, I suppose, ain't they."

He leaned for his stool, then started off, but stopped to face me again. "Mart, we ain't to forget there was good in your brother," he said, and in both confusion and relief, I watched his back away, til I blundered off toward the flank of my next lady.

I gazed out the window beyond. Til a minute later I felt the sweep of a tail at my hip and looked down into two patient eyes, and the wonder behind them at why I hadn't begun to relieve her swelling.

"So Bossie!" I said. "What *you* been up to today?"

Father let me off early, as he sometimes did when we were done drawing down the cows. He said he'd finish up on his own. And in the storm's aftermath, he thought the fish would be biting; and perhaps I might see if I could bring up a couple for breakfast.

The light was gray and misty as I started toward the house, but something caught my eye and I turned to see a figure up by the roadside some distance away. A woman holding a handbag.

Not a woman, but *Isis!* Looking back.

I stared, then threw up an arm and broke toward her at a run.

She was wet all through, with her hair and gown both clinging.

"What in holy hell!" I said, halting.

Her chin rose. "I told you," she said. "I'm going away. I need some clothes, Marty! And I gotta have you cut my hair."

"Jesus Mary!" I cried.

I shot glances up the road and down. Nothing. Through the mist, only the dull glow of Mama's flowers in the bed by the porch steps. When I looked back Isis had shifted and my eye caught on a purplish smudge at her cheek.

I pointed. "What's *that*!"

She shook her head. "Can you *help* me, Marty!"

I kept staring at the bruise.

"Will you!" she said. "Can I stay in the loft just tonight?"

She stood there patiently. My heart wrenched. I looked past her into the orchard below and took a few moments to breathe myself still. I didn't know what to do, then heard myself blurt, "Down there!" I pointed and motioned her to follow. We went cross lot, where I left her under a tree. I hurried to the house and ten minutes later returned with a towel, a pear, and an end cut of fresh bread, having paused to consider how I'd explain that to Mama.

After supper I found Mama's long shears and wrapped them in a pair of linen trousers and a plain muslin pullover. Linen would have been more durable than the cotton, and cooler in the summer heat, but the two shirts I held up were too small, even approaching their limit with me. I slid an old felt hat and the bundle under my bed. I had forced myself not to think. Not to think!

It was near seven o'clock when I was able to get into the pantry again. I folded a dinner napkin about bread slices, a block of cheese, and a cut of pie. I left the house when I saw Father go out behind the barn, carrying tools and a fence post.

I looked at the barn as we readied ourselves for the dash upslope. Swallows dipped in from beyond toward our destination in the barn's upper reaches.

We hurried in, past the milk room and down the steps to where the light by the grain bin was already poor. There was none at all when I turned into the narrow shaft leading up. I put my shoulder to the sidewall and leaned into the steepness.

The air was sweet with the scent of hay and for an instant I recalled the old times when Jerry and Alf and once or twice Isis herself would leap and shriek gleefully from the crossbeams into the mountain of hay we'd piled up below. We'd named these plunges "T-dives" after the shape of our bodies and outspread arms.

Such a world it was then! The rapture, coiling and leaping, out far and soaring and plunging in deep; to scramble out and up again into the heights. It felt now as if we'd been plunged into some fairy tale. Like Hansel and Gretel!

What murky light to be had came from a row of small square windows set high above the floor in the east wall. We settled ourselves toward the far end and I brought out what I'd gathered for her.

She said she didn't know what she'd do if she didn't have me. Then she ate and we were still, and when she'd finished—I had been dreading this—she took up the scissors. She held them up for a second, then out to me and turned away to sit on her legs.

I stood on my knees and worked in close. My fingers slid up her neck. I lifted out the mass of her and held it, having no idea how to begin, how much to take.

"Don't fuss," she said. "Just cut it all. Short."

It went quickly, and within minutes all that remained was an inch or two of stubble all around. Her neck was milky, her head now only a dark globe. I looked at what I'd set aside and asked did she want to save any. She laughed, said she'd get it back some day, then she turned around on her bottom, though only part way and not enough to face me.

For a minute neither of us spoke. But then, when are eyes met, and held, it was like a dam breaking and in the same instant we burst out laughing.

Then we froze. *How had we allowed it?*

I think of it now and I wonder how things might have gone differently if that outburst had not happened. But perhaps it was the only defense we had then: to laugh in the face of the grotesque.

And I think that in some way we both knew we'd cut off far more than her hair!

At length she whispered that I'd done good, and while she finished the last of her meal, I brought out the poem I had copied out boldly enough to be read in the gloom. I told her about Robert's visit and the letter and something of the aftermath, including Frank's visit.

She took a while with the poem and at last looked up, but not at me.

"It's so beautiful. So sad," she whispered, then took a few seconds before turning to face me fully. "But Marty, I'm not the one should be reading this."

My shoulder jerked.

"It's for her," she said. "You should give it to *her*!"

I sagged.

"Some day, don't you think?"

I looked away, alarmed, but then couldn't contain myself.

I snarled. "Sure! OH SURE!"

Everything within and about us seized.

For a minute we scarcely breathed. Then I whispered I'd better go in. But I didn't stir. And we were quiet til I asked where she thought to go in the morning.

"Keene," she said. "Keene first, then ⋯ just west."

I gaped.

"There's people, there'll be some," she said. Then she reminded me of the gold piece her mother had given her.

I looked at her in awe. All she faced!. All she *had* faced! And here with such simple receiving.

Then all at once the back of my neck prickled and a call came up the staircase.

"Marty! Is that you up there?"

NINE

"Sam, all I *know* is that girl needs help. A woman *knows* these things!"

"And I know we ain't got two dollars a week. Don't that settle it?"

It was an hour later, and I was straining to hear, leaning down over my knees from as low as I dared to sit on the staircase. Father was seated, I'd determined, but I could tell that Mama was pacing about. "Well I am settled on this," she said. "I ain't taking her back!"

"You know well as I that danged fellow up there's half crazy, apt to come down with a shotgun on his arm." There was a long silence til he spoke again. "All right then, in the morning I'll take it to the constable. "We'll let him deal with it."

"Not yet, no. Let me see if Reverend Caswell can't find something for her. I will do that first."

Another silence, "Well, I better to talk to that fella, too, then. I'll go up there first thing and see if he ain't interested in a steady dollar or two a week."

I heard Father come out of his chair and stood to retreat to my room, where I'd been banished with very few words after our return to the house. Isis had been put in the spare bedroom downstairs off the far end of the parlor. It was small space, rarely entered and with barely enough room to stand, let alone move about. Ned had occasionally brought classmates home from college during holidays, and two or three times a year Aunt Marion came down from Concord for a few days. To me it hardly existed, but I kept seeing Isis, sitting against the wall on the narrow bed just looking and looking out the window.

It was half hour til Mama came up to me. She wasn't angry. She didn't dwell on my 'unthinkable poor judgment'. There'd be time for that later. But it surprised me to hear that she was proud of me for trying to help. She asked me no questions and didn't stay long. Perhaps she already knew far more than I could reveal, and in any case, the hard look in her eyes that told me she'd been roused to something important.

I tried to imagine Isis as a hired girl but couldn't hold the image of her going about some house in the village in a maid's cap and apron. And for much of the time before I fell asleep it kept roiling about in my head.

Take it to her sometime!

. . .

Mama usually wakened me on the few occasions when I required it in the morning, but the next day it was Father's hand that gripped my shoulder. He told me he needed me early, that was all, then turned and went out.

I came downstairs to find Mama seated in the chair nearest the spare bedroom door, still in her night clothes and carpet slippers. She raised a forefinger to her lips. On the table beside her was an empty tumbler and the remaining inch or two of candle she'd snuffed out.

Father said almost nothing as we worked the cows in the barn, before he withdrew "on an errand" and left me to tidy up on my own. Breakfast was later than usual and the three of us ate mostly in silence. Mama left shortly after herself, after having me confirm her instructions to stay at my tasks and out of the house til she returned.

At midmorning I stood behind Father in the tool shed as he mixed a bucket of turkey red. Then he sent me off to scrape and paint the cellar entry on the south side of the house. But on the way, I angled across to peer in the kitchen window. They were together with their backs to me at the sink. Isis' head was tied up in a bandana, but it nearly brought me a grin, seeing all the folds and pins it had taken to get her up in one of Mama's gowns.

At my work later I stole around back. I'd heard the two of them go out some time before, most likely with the wash basket. But now they were out beyond under the wide cloudless sky picking berries. For a minute or two I watched their movements, a row apart, backs to me and in grave silence as it seemed.

The four of us came together for the first time at lunch. Mama and Isis took seats, while I stood with Father til he soberly concluded the grace. "... ever mindful of our walk with thee, on this day, and all our days to come. Amen." It was same consecration I'd heard at every meal, every day of my life. "Amen," Mama and I whispered in concert.

Isis kept her head lowered. Between us were platters of pork, green beans, and sliced potatoes giving up wisps of steam; a pitcher of milk; bread and butter. "Martin helped with the jam," Mama said brightly, but Isis offered no response.

Mama looked up at me, then at Father. "Well, you two. Now you've begun with some painting outside, I wonder if you might get on with the rest of the house."

Father leaned back, then rubbed a little showingly at his chin. "Well now, since you mention it, I notice Marty ain't been goin' to school these days."

Isis peered up from the tops of her eyes as I reached for the potatoes. I said I was thinking of going back.

"No need of that," quipped Father, "not if you've a mind to keep goin' with that brush!"

Mama turned. "You have to be hungry, dear!" she said. But Isis only closed her eyes and drew a breath. "All right then," Mama went on, shifting in her seat, "perhaps ⋯ perhaps it might help if we tell you what we've found?"

Isis looked up, and out past my shoulder.

"We think we can find you a place to stay. Mr. Croslin is agreed to it, Martin's father has been out to see him and I ..."

Isis looked at her in alarm.

"Oh my dear girl, we do need to think about this. We just cannot have ..."

"It won't do, mum." Her voice was low and hoarse, but firm.

"What's that, dear?"

Into the silence a fly buzzed at the window.

"Isis. My dear. There's no other way, you're here now and I must . . ."

"He changes. He won't go for it."

"Oh, I think he will." Mama straightened, her eyes alight. "I think he will unless he wants this taken to the constable." Isis shrank into her chair but Mama went on. "That's what we've told him and we are determined to see this through."

Isis' chin fell to her chest. "It's trouble," she murmured. "I don't want no more."

Mama turned to her and leaned in.

"My dear girl, trouble is what we've *got*! And we are not going to have it continue."

. . .

The next morning I was sent out to scrub the stanchions, and with a stiff brush and a bucket of wood-ash soap, I labored two hours or more before Father came in to consider my efforts. He said it was good work and looked me up and down, from my sweat-streaked face to my clinging linens, then told me to go down for a swim if I wanted. "Go on," he said. "Clean yourself up, if nothin' else."

At mid-afternoon I was in the tool room, having shifted, back and forth, all manner of boxes, saws, hammers, bars, picks, rakes, hoes, shovels - even the racks of scrap wood - to sweep the shelves and then the floor. When at last I went out to the pump for a drink, I could hear Mama keeping up a steady chatter with - or at - Isis in the kitchen. I thought how she'd never had a girl to share her long days. I went to the window. Isis had an apron tied over a pale blue gown spotted with small blossoms. Mama left the stove and crossed to the pantry, where she stopped in the entry and stood for a minute with her back to me. When she turned, her face was soft and sad - but also radiant in a way that brought my heart a sudden lurch. I drew back and watched as she brisked at her hair and squared herself up before returning to Isis.

I watched her adjust her apron, straighten and square herself, brush at her cheek and take a long breath.

I turned back toward the barn in awe at the terrible fusion of opposites I'd seen in my mother's face. And then, when I was scarcely through the tool room door, I was halted by a surge of emotion - to do something for her!

I stared across at the heaps of spare lumber on the shelves.

A box! I could make a box, something square and simple. Of pine. That would be easiest to sand and nail up, though I would have preferred cherry or walnut. I had no skill with saw and hammer, even if, through Father I had come to appreciate wood in all its potential, in the subtlety of its grains and the polished hues of finished work.

For the better part of the next hour, I lost myself in the effort, measuring and cutting a six-inch rectangle, then four others uniformly smaller. Only then did I pause and come to terms with the fact that I couldn't finish it this day, especially since I wanted shellac and varnish. I sanded the edges, began tacking it up, and thought about showing it to Mama unfinished. I decided to wait, but I think the box had already done some of its work— for me at least!

I went outside, still thinking of Mama and all that had fallen on her. I thought of the girl she'd lost at only three, and of my walks up cemetery hill with her every April to stand with her by the little stone. She told me Marcia was with God in Heaven, and so at an early age I understood that Marcia wasn't really dead. And I had wondered if Marcia was still three or if she was growing older every year like I was.

I wandered around out back and sat against the house in the shade. But almost at once Isis came around the corner to say they'd seen me go past and that Mama wanted me to come in for a treat. Her apron was spotted red here and there from the berries they'd gathered earlier, or perhaps from some work in the kitchen. She came on a few more steps and halted. Then her face changed.

"Marty, what am I gonna do?" she pleaded. "*What?*"

I sat, open-mouthed.

"She's been so *good* to me, but I can't do this!"

I looked at my feet. She said she was sorry and then took a minute to gather herself. Then she shifted.

"I heard about your little sister," she said. "She told me about the accident, the one with the wagon."

"Marcia? She told you that? She never talks about Marcia, only when she makes a cake every year on her birthday."

She looked down at me a moment - and almost smiled, as it seemed. "Don't you wonder about her name?" she asked.

I puzzled.

"Ain't it a little like yours?"

"No! It ain't."

"She told me something, you know. She said she didn't want any more children. Not for a long time, but then you came along and she was glad."

"Well I ain't named for her," I said, annoyed. I stood. "There's some letters in it is all." I started off and passed her at a pace.

"But I guess there *is* another girl now," she called after. "The one with that woman!"

I swung hard around the back corner and went up alongside the house at a clip. *Another girl!*

Then at the front corner—just there at the corner—something took me wholly unbidden. I spun about and flung it at her. "All right! Why don't we go up there! You and me!"

It was a dead shock to us both.

She said she couldn't. And I couldn't. I couldn't leave Mama now, not after Ned.

"But that's what I said to *you!* About leaving *your* mother!" I looked down at one of my hands shaking.

"It ain't the *same thing*, Marty!"

I could see she was close to tears and yet I kept on. I said she was right about that girl, and the poem and the woman.

We stood facing each for a while til the tension eased.

And in the end it may have been that Isis knew she would not stay herself and that here, at least, was a way out. I said I'd leave a letter so's they'd know it wasn't she that caused it.

TEN

We managed a short exchange after supper. She said she was used to sleeping like a cat and to knock three times, then once more. I went into Ned's room to rummage around in his chiffonier til I found the red bandana he sometimes wore. The faint scent of him in it pulled at me; I wondered what he'd think of its use now. I worked on the letter in my room, stopping once to let a rush of terror subside and recalling what Ned had once written about going into a battle: Of course you were afraid of going in, but your mates expected it of you - and even more, you expected it of yourself! I filled two pages, with arrows pointing here and there—and as many cross-outs as acceptable lines. Then I took a pen and copied it out.

My dear Mother and Father,
I have wanted to find out about that little girl in Canada. So I decided to do that. I will meet them I hope, and then come back and tell you about it. I will not go for very long. And this is <u>not</u> Isis's idea, it is mine. She is going too, <u>but she is not to blame</u>. She didn't want to but said if it would help she would go. Also she said Mr. Croslin will NOT LET HER STAY HERE. So she can help me and I will help her.

I looked at the map for how to go. We are going first over to Keene and then over to Albany, NY to take the cars over there. We have some money for the fare but it's not any I took, honest. I promise you that.

Mama, this is helping Isis and she thinks so too or she wouldn't do it. (She is pretty strong just like you said) She said to thank you so much, and Father too, WHICH I KNOW SHE REALLY MEANS. So don't worry because I will come back after a few days.

From your loving son,
Martin

There was only one fib, but it was a big one. For Father. I said we were going to Keene, but in fact we were going east, in the opposite direction, up Butternut Mountain and down the other side to look for rides into Manchester. From there we would take the cars north, hoping that Isis's ten-dollar gold piece would cover the fare to Montreal.

I tried not to think of the morrow and all help we would need, and all the fibbing. I thought of the girl in Canada and if she might look like Ned. I thought of Mama meeting her sometime.

I went to the window at eleven, after the soft strokes from the parlor clock below went still. The moon was a bright quarterly hanging in the southwest sky. The night was clear and dry and full of high stars. I sat gazing into the stillness, with the only stir being the slow in and out of my breath. I let myself go to its calming effect. Maybe I was meant to do this. Maybe we two were. All these events, one after another, hadn't they all found their way to this? I felt myself carried along, as if in some dark river, like our own out back. I thought of my little friend, the mallard.

And then once again I panicked. *What if Mama...*

I squeezed my eyes tight shut and shook my head.

. . .

Isis waited behind on the porch, while I paused in the open doorway with my shoes hooked in the fingers of one hand. I took a last impression, running my gaze over the big cookstove, past the sinks and counters and the door to the pantry to linger for a moment on Mama's empty chair beyond the table. Then I turned out into the night.

We exchanged a quick, somber glance, then started diagonally across the lawn The air was sharp and cool. Feet returned munching sounds on the road, our shadows kept pace ahead. Isis walked tall with her head up. The shirt and broadcloth trousers fit her passingly well. The straw hat was a little too big, but then, it hid more of her. Only one thing had given me pause: The shoes were her own; my Sunday pair wouldn't do and were too big in the bargain. Still, hers were worn badly enough, and if she kept the pant legs well down . . .

At the top of the rise I stopped and turned for a last look at the dark shapes of the house and barn below.

"Okay, Marty?" she asked.

"Yeah, I think so."

We were fifteen minutes to the head of the village green. The upper half of our church steeple caught the moonlight, but the gray mass below loomed ghostly. We passed it by and went down the east side road, where the yard gates were all snugly latched, the houses all dark behind except for one near the end where an oil lamp within cast a dim amber glow. And at last we turned into what struck me as our true point of departure.

The lower shoulders of Butternut Mountain were open and pastured, but after a half mile the town road turned to wagon ruts separated by narrow, grassy lanes. And soon then, the way began to steepen and the forest to crowd in close. We were without shadow now, and all ahead looked forbiddingly deep and black. I thought of spirits, though I didn't believe in spirits. Didn't think I did.

To Isis, of course, this was familiar territory; she'd returned up here many a time alone. I thought of passing by the crude lane ahead that led off to her world, such as it was. I wondered, but didn't ask, how she'd feel. We'd both found it easiest to keep to ourselves. I thought of her mother. I couldn't recall her name, if I'd ever heard it. I had only seen her once or twice, and not for a while. I had studied her once from a little distance as she sat in their cart outside Wilson's store. She'd never looked left or right, but only held a kind of vacant smile while gazing out ahead. She had a narrow, weathered face and thin hair that hung beyond her shoulders. I'd always been afraid to ask Isis about her, and Isis had only ever responded to the jibes at school with stony silence.

I looked up to the wedge of sky between the trees ahead. We'd be another hour to the summit, or more, but the descent into Francestown would be faster. I hoped we might get there before sunrise. I searched my mind for someone, for a family acquaintance, from whom we might have to duck out of sight. Then all at once I realized that Isis had dropped from my side. I was five or six strides beyond when I halted and turned to see her by an opening I'd entirely missed! I went back and stood by as she looked down into the narrow, rough-tracked lane.

"I wish I could take her with me," she said over her shoulder, but evenly, without any particular emotion, and not asking for a response as it seemed. But I moved in a step. She bent and twisted up some of the long grass and stood with it in her hand for few seconds, then let it go and turned.

But I'd noticed something I had to mention. "Only one thing," I said. "That ain't a boy's way, you can't bend down sidewise like that." She looked at me and returned a half smile.

On and on we went, trudging upward for two hours or more wrapped in darkness. But at last the night opened wide all around and the sky deepened wondrously into a dome filled with tiny points of light.

Fifty years earlier the top of Butternut Mountain had been burned off in a great fire, leaving the whole summit to the elements and the eventual loss of most of its soil. What remained was a vast, bald granite ledge that, before us now, was bathed all in silver save for a few shadowy pockets here and there. We stopped to gaze - and all at once a long-lost verse sprang up in my head.

What makes silver, what makes gray,
What makes Johnny come out to play.

Isis found a patch of grass; I settled into a smooth hollow a short ways above. I looked up into the stars, and at length two or three came to feel little eyes. I recalled a book Sunbeam had lent me, *Uncle Tom's Cabin*, and then I looked about for the Big Dipper, thinking of the two in the story who had followed it north. I pictured them and their struggle and for a moment thought how our own didn't seem so bad after all.

It was five minutes or so til Isis turned to say something I couldn't quite make out. But there was something hard in her voice that made me sit up. "What's that?" I said.

"I said I almost *did* it!" She was looking sideways, up and out into the night.

"Did what?"

" I could have. I had the ax!"

"WHAT! You had WHAT?"

"But they'd take me off and then she'd have no one."

"Jumpers! An ax!"

"I watched him sleeping, I could've done it!" she said and turned to look at me. "I could smell it on him, Marty, that stuff he makes." I sat agape. "Instead I decided to leave," she said. Then she rose. She said there were things I didn't know and started up to pass me by while I only sat, staring, with my heart in my throat.

I stood and followed, stumbling along, four five six paces behind with my head full of unspeakable imaginings. And she kept on in haste til we well were over the top and beyond before slowing.

The eastern slope was longer but not as steep, and being more open, there was more light. We followed our long shadows, and after a while I began to think of the rides we'd need. We had a story ready and had agreed that Isis wouldn't speak unless she had to. I thought of the questions we'd surely get and voiced answers to myself. The first pearly light began to bleed in, then the road flattened and improved but remained empty. Manchester was still a good twenty-five miles away.

Stone walls began to frame us, and a light mist hung low over the pastures and fields beyond. The sky came in blue and clear. When we stopped to for something to eat, my stomach began to churn, though not hunger. I had never been good at lying but tried to convince myself that it was mostly to do with Father, who'd always been able to look right through me to a fib. I could hear him.

Honest, my hat! Turn out yer pockets!

The first wagon came along, and I flashed a glance at Isis before hopping down. I waved, put on a smile, and stood watching the man's face as he kept it set ahead and passed by. Isis laughed. She said she didn't want to ride with him anyway.

Another flatbed came along, driven by an older man in red suspenders. I felt a little easier now and waited longer, til it seemed just the right moment to raise a casual arm and hail with proper restraint.

The man reined in. He was indeed an elderly fellow, with thick gray eyebrows and a heavily creased face. But in the bright suspenders, and with his straw-hat tipped well back, he looked amiable enough.

"Morning boys!" he said, raising two knuckly fingers toward the rim of his hat. "And a fine one, too, if I don't say. What can I do for ya?"

"If you please, sir," I began, feeling myself like an actor on a stage. "My mother's taken sick, and we been sent up to the city to fetch my aunt."

"Where you headed? Manchester?"

"Yes sir," I said. "That's right."

The man's eyes cut to Isis, then back. "That far," he said.

"Yes, sir. We came from Hancock just now. Up on Norway Hill, if you know it."

"Well now, that's a little distance, ain't it. What's ailing yer momma?"

"It's her stomach, sir. Doctor said she needs a woman's help more than just my father and me."

"Ayuh. And who would it be I'm talkin' to, then?"

"Ned Roberts, sir. And this here's my cousin Jimmy."

The man took a few moments to look us over, first Isis, then me. Then he looked ahead and considered.

"Wal. I'm goin' far as Goffstown if that'll help you any."

I thanked him heartily and turned a quick grin at Isis.

"Abel Blinn," said our fellow. "That's me," he said and assumed a mock frown. "But don't go callin' me Abe, ya' hear."

"No sir!" I said, knowing full well what he meant, even if he didn't strike me as having Father's political leanings.

I climbed onto the seat beside him, while Isis went around back to boost herself behind into the empty bed.

"Now you tell me something, You two ain't out skylarking, are ye, when ye ought to be in school?"

I allowed a hint of indignation in my denial and said the summer session had already ended.

"On a farm are ya'?" he asked.

I told him we were; I said we had nineteen cows just then. "Most of them are like those over there," I said, pointing to a cluster of Holsteins beyond a wall just ahead, two or three of them already regarding us with languid eyes. "Ayuh," returned Mr. Blinn. And as we passed by he dipped his head at a near full grown heifer. "Bossie," he said.

And now he began a steady chatter. First it was milk cows. The Ayrshire was the finest, he thought, though you didn't see many of them til you got closer to the city and the more prosperous farms. Then he went on to tell how they didn't keep up these county roads the way they used to, and how everything got managed better when he was a younger fellow. "Churches, houses, fences and all that. Before this durn war come on." He paused. "But I don't s'pose you want yer ear bent over *that*!"

Now we heard that he had a bad back and how it didn't do so well in the wagon. Nor his bum knees, neither, while sittin' long stretches in the wagon. And he guessed we wouldn't mind if he had to stop off a minute or two to stretch himself.

When he went quiet for a time, I thought of Mama and imagined her fretting about in the house. And Father. He'd be making inquiries out on the road somewhere, or perhaps in Peterborough by now.

"I've got three grandsons, m'self," Mr. Blinn mused, and I turned to nod, expecting more, but we jostled along in silence for a short while - til he pointed to a five-foot-wide stream that had come in alongside. "Now this here's the Piscataquog," he said. "Nicest little trout river you'll ever find. And I'll tell ya, when I was a lad of your age . . ."

And so it went until we came into Goffstown Village and stopped in front of a grain storehouse.

"End of the line for me boys," said Mr. Blinn as he turned to me with a grin. "And none too soon for you, I expect, seein' as I 'bout talked the flowers off the both of ya." I disputed it vigorously, sincerely, and he said, "Wal, ye'll forgive an old fellow, anaway."

We climbed down, and I don't think Isis had spoken two words, especially as I'd done my best to preclude it. But when we were done with our last thanks, Mr. Blinn slid over on the bench. He leaned in toward Isis and broke a kindly smile.

"Now young lady," he said with a twinkle in his eye. "I'm gonna give you some advice. Next time, if I was you, I'd do something about those shoes."

Isis stiffened. My mouth fell open.

"All right now," he said, raising a hand. "I don't know what yer up to, but ye both seem proper to me." Then he sat back and went into a pocket. "I want you stayin' out of trouble," he said, still struggling with his hand.

He held out his arm, not to me but to Isis.

"Take this," he said. Take it. Ain't much, but I want you usin' it proper."

Isis looked at the coin in her hand, then up again at Mr. Blinn. She held his eye, then thanked him quietly; but the slight soft smile that followed said more.

ELEVEN

She didn't react to my wonder at such a simple older fellow; I said I didn't think he'd even seen the shoes. "He didn't," she said. "He looked around at me. He did that three times, and I could tell his back hurt, too, when he did. Anyway, he saw some things, but it's all right. Most people won't."

There was plenty of traffic now, and I felt confident of our prospects. We started off out of the village and walked for a short while before taking a break under an elm, with a slight easterly breeze adding to its welcome shade. I handed Isis a baked potato. For a brief while we watched as an eagle circled lazily about high above, its head gleaming in the sun, and I wondered at its remove from all the troubles in the world below.

We were both thirsty, and when I stood down by the road then moved left a few paces into a cloud-shadow, I thought of a new approach. Two fellows shook their heads. Then a larger, express wagon came along.

"Sir," I hailed. "Would you have anything to drink you could share?"

The wagon slowed, and it surprised me to see that the driver was a young chap not many years older than me. He leaned in toward me - his cheeks were pockmarked - and through an open window in a heavy Irish accent called out.

"Sorry lads."

The wagon passed on. *C. George & Co., No. 14* it said in bold crimson on the side panel.

But then it halted. An arm waved us on. I shot a look at Isis, then ran up alongside to find the driver slid over toward us. He held out a clay jug. We each took pulls, but when I reached it back he swept the back of his hand at us. "No, no, take some more. Much as ye like."

He was a wiry, smallish fellow, though I began to feel him larger as he kept a steady gaze throughout, studying us as we indulged. And with his hand at rest on the door, I noticed where he had gnawed at the nails of a finger and thumb. "Would'ya be needing a lift then, lads?" he said at last, but with a trace of slyness that gave me a charge.

He said his name was Mick when we were underway. But after I told him ours he stayed silent for a long while. The blinkered, gray mare drew us along at a fair pace, and as the time went voicelessly on and on, I felt increasingly cramped and uncomfortable. I could sense it in Isis, too, and at last I said he could just drop us off anywhere now and we'd be obliged.

He kept his eyes ahead. "We ain't there yet."

We came up on a long, finely-fitted a rock wall fronting a large and prosperous farm. There were more wagons now, more people afoot, houses set closer together. And then storefronts, at one of which, in his loose-fitting blouse and faded maroon knee pants Mick stopped to stroll off with a parcel under his arm. Isis said she didn't like this fellow *at all!* But I knew we were close; I could hear the low, steady rumble of the Merrimac River Falls ahead. Then the city heights came into view, and not long after the road curved to reveal ahead the opening to a massive covered bridge.

"Here we be, lads!" he said, then he turned with a glint in his eye. "But that there bridge, it ain't a safe crossin' for runaways!"

"We ain't runaways!" Isis said, flaring.

I pointed ahead and said my aunt was expecting us. "Up there on that hill," I said. He ignored me.

"Acros't that bridge the coppers are gonna nab ya sure."

I threw Isis a panicky look. Her eyes had narrowed, her mouth was pressed tight.

Suddenly our youth sat up and directed the wagon into a side road. He snapped the reins. "Don't worry, lads. This way's best," he said as we began bumping along on a rough road crowded in on the right by dreary, flat-roofed wooden dwellings set close together, and on the left by another long row, but this of brick warehouses. We came up on a rutted intersection and slowed.

"We'll get off here," I shrilled.

Not a word. Only his blank face fixed ahead.

"Stop!" snapped Isis. "Stop here!"

"Sit tight, mate. Si-t tight!"

A scrawny dog raced in, yapping and keeping up alongside, til our fellow slowed a little, reached down and then tossed a small bone out the window. "Don't need noon a' that now, do we."

Isis elbowed me hard. I looked at her; did she want to jump? I sat rigid.

What passed for houses gave way to even sorrier dwellings, unpainted shanties set side to side behind shallow, barren yards. There was no one about. We slowed again and the youth held up a small metal whistle. He said his mother lived just ahead and whenever he gave a toot she'd come out for a greet. He drew the wagon up and sent out three quick shrieks. Then we stopped.

I heard a baby behind a nearby wall—also, from somewhere ahead, the sound of a musical instrument. Isis elbowed me again. I turned to see a boy in the alley between two houses. He came on and began looking about as if for others.

Isis leaned across. "What's this goin' on?"

He frowned and only watched the boy coming along. And then there *were* others, one, two, then three more scruffy young fellows. They drew in together and advanced.

"Ooh. Be jimmed if it ain't them nasty little McGillivrays!"

One was older and better dressed, in a waist-jacket and a tweed cap set at a jaunty angle. The others were younger than me, thin and angular, all with wrists and ankles out the ends of tattered shirts and trousers. They came up, stopped and set hands into fists at their hips.

"All right, boys, end of the line. Now y'cn stand down!"

The older one looked up at us in disdain. "What's this?" he said to Mick. "Girlies now?"

"Now 'Arold, be nice," said the youth. He elbowed my shoulder. "Stan' doon now an joos do as yer told." When we didn't move, he leaned across and jabbed an arm past Isis at the door.

The wagon lurched away, leaving us staring into pale faces and wolfish eyes.

"Let's 'av yer coppers," said the older one, "whatever ye got, then you go. Fair enoof?"

"Do we look like we're full of money?" said Isis.

"Look 'ere. We doon't want to hurt ye."

The smaller ones edged in with eyes and hands at the ready.

I hadn't much to lose. Only the pocket knife. But she did! Mr. Blinn's quarter dollar and *The eagle!* Our railroad fare,

"One way or another," said the boy. "We got more help if we need it."

The older one picked up my knife and my handkerchief. He opened the page with Ned's poem on it, grimaced, and flipped it aside. "Yer turn," he said to Isis,

She went to one pocket and turned it out. Nothing. Then the other. Again nothing. *Nothing at all from her!*

The tall boy looked at her in disgust. "All right then. Let's 'av yer shoes."

Isis shook her head. The boy ignored her and turned to me. "Yoors, too. An' be quick aboot it, you two ain't worth spit!"

"I ain't takin' off my shoes," Isis said coldly, which brought a few ooh's of derision.

Was it their hoots of derision, the mockery of these mites that all at once aroused me? Or was it more to do with Isis and the implacable defiance of a girl!

I ain't either!" I said.

The older boy scanned the faces of his mates, then slowly raised a hand; and when his fingers snapped all the bodies came rushing in. One leaped up high, another struck me at the waist, and a third piled on when I went down. They were like furies. Hands and fingers raked at me. And all at once a searing pain by my ankle.

But then a loud cry from one of them five feet away. "This one's a GIRLIE!"

And then they were gone, and I watched the last of them disappear as I gripped at the pain in my foot. Isis shouted something, and then we, too, were up and scrambling.

But at fifty yards off I halted. *The poem!*

I said I had to go back.

Five minutes later we stood on the west bank of the river gazing two hundred feet across at a wall of many-windowed, five-story brick buildings that ran as far downstream as we could see. *What were we to do now!*

But my throbbing ankle demanded attention; I told Isis I needed to go down and chill it in the water. And when I looked back at her sitting in the grass a few minutes later and saw her holding her shirt together, it struck me that she'd been doing that all along; it had been torn through all down the front!

She drew her knees up as I approached and wrapped them in her arms. Then, as if she'd read my thoughts -or my face - she said she was thinking how to find another shirt. I told her we'd exchange but she shook her head.

The clatter of machinery in the mills began to subside, and then over the river came several shrill blasts of a whistle.

Noon. *Noon!* It seemed like a notion from another world.

And now I saw the straw hat! Still on her head!

She said they left it when they ran, then opened a hand. "And we still got these."

Jesus! the coins!

She smiled. "I didn't fight any. I just made like a turtle."

"Yeah but ··· how?"

She shook her head forcefully and then looked me in the eye - til all at once I cut away, blushing.

. . .

We made our way along the south wall of the bridge on a four-foot pedestrian walk, gazing through the spacing between the planks at the swirling current below. Beside us passed wagons and carriages on sets of raised tracks. On the east bank, we paused to look up into the city center. Just ahead was a young man in a soldier's kepi and faded army coat. One of his legs was missing below the knee, and he leaned on a cane, holding out a tin cup. My eyes caught his briefly as we went by, and a few paces on I found myself thinking of Ned - and then how this fellow's luck hadn't been *all bad*. after all; I wondered if he knew that.

Elm Street was a mile from the squalid Irish district to which we'd been delivered, but it might have been on another continent. It was a boulevard! Straight from the pages of *Harper's Weekly*: triple wide, cobblestone paved, long and flat and perfectly straight, with trolley tracks gleaming down the center into the distance. Well-dressed people bustled or strolled leisurely about: men in suits and top hats, women holding fringed parasols against the sun; glossy carriages and handsome horses.

We went down a short ways and stood into a narrow space between two buildings. In our tatters and bare feet, we could ask for nothing here, but we needed a short pause to reassure ourselves in witness of such an orderly realm as this. I looked at the signs in or above the shop windows across the way.

A. Jones, Furrier; *Oils & Liniments*; *Paper Hanging & Upholstering.*

We returned to cross the busy intersection and head uphill, having decided to look for a house with a woman about. We passed through another intersection and then a large square bordered by imposing three-story houses. These too seemed beyond us in our current state, but soon enough the dwellings became smaller and set closer together. At one we stopped to consider a sign in the corner of a front window.

Ames Boarding House
Jews, Negroes welcome.
No Irish.

"No Irish!" I said and chuckled. "Hey, we might get some help here!" I drew myself up as if before an open door and said, "Excuse me, madam. We just got ruffed about by a gang of Irish and I was wondering ... "

"I'll do it!" said Isis, and not waiting for a reaction she turned up the brick walk, pausing on the porch to look back at me before pulling the clapper and stepping back to wait. I went to stand against the trunk of a nearby maple.

The door opened to a full-figured woman of about Mama's age. I watched a brief exchange before she came out a step, then squinted a little to hold her unchanging regard as she listened for two or three minutes - until Isis took off her hat, at which the woman straightened as her hand went to her mouth. My hopes leapt, and another minute went by, then the woman turned sideways and beckoned Isis in!

Fifteen minutes or more passed, and I'd begun circling about in the road when I looked up to see the door open and Isis emerge in a gray denim shirt! The woman followed her out. Her face was warm. She looked out and raised me a hearty wave I returned at once.

There were shoes, too, a little large but passable - and an extra pair of socks, as it turned out. The woman followed Isis out to the edge of the porch and called out to me. "I'm gonna *hear* from her now. And don't you let her forget!"

And then we were away, and glowing. At least I was.

"I just told her!" Isis said a little wryly, as if I ought to have known. "I just said what happened. And all about you and where we were going. And she told me some things, too. She said her husband lost his job. She said the Irish took it for cheap!" And as we made our way back downhill I heard that the woman had a son, her only child, in the army, and that the shirt and boots were from a chest of his earlier belongings. She'd said she'd thought they might be needed someday, though the fellow hadn't had a sweetheart in a while!

At one point Isis's step hitched and for a second she winced. But at once she held up a packet the woman had also left with her, and we paused to enjoy one of the chunky, apple-filled squares.

I said they were as good as Mama's at home. "Even better," I said. "Funny thing about the Irish. First they're all bad luck, and then maybe because of them it helps around the other way."

Isis didn't suppose it was any luck at all.

TWELVE

I began to think about shops. The woman had told about one by the depot that sold small meat pies. She hadn't known about the train fare, but she thought two dollars would get me a pair of shoes. But when we were about half way along, I noticed that Isis had begun to slow, and when she fell back another few feet, I turned to see her in some slight discomfort. But maybe just fatigue.

We stopped in the depot's north entrance to take in the vast interior: a deep, dimly lit and seemingly empty hall with a thirty-foot opening to the boarding platform on the right. Against the brick wall on the left was a row of high-backed oaken benches, where I made out three figures seated alone, and nearest us a woman with a small child. I turned. "Good," I said. "There ain't much going on this time of day."

I squinted. In the light of a gaslamp behind a grid at the far end sat our object, the ticket agent. I went on two or three steps til I could make out a bald-headed fellow, apparently at some reading. The clock on the wall above said it was nearly three. Off to the right stood the schedule board. I pointed that way and we set off, then slowed at the sound of our footfalls.

There were five or six entries in the northbound column, but my eye went right to the bottom. **Montreal Night Express, 8:03 P.M.**

Five hours. *Or a whole lot more!*

Isis stood behind me as I drew myself up and waited. The agent stayed at his newspaper. I shifted and it brought nothing. "Excuse me, sir," I said. "Could you tell me the fare to Montreal."

He looked up, slowly, and poked at his silver-rimmed spectacles. He was an older fellow with a broad face and a bump on his nose. "That far, ey?" he said. "And in your bare feet, too!"

My shoulders drew in. "No-o!" I stammered. "I'm gonna get some!"

"Gonna get some," he said, expressionless.

"Yes, sir. Mine . . . See, I saw this soldier and he was begging

The man held a sharp eye on me. "Sure you are," he said. "And it was an old pair, anyway, I suppose."

"Pretty worn sir, I guess. Yes sir."

He sighed. "Son, you're not much of a liar, anyone ever tell you that?" My eyes dropped, and for a moment I stood, mute. But all at once I flooded full of bitterness. At him. At all of it. *Everything!*

"You wouldn't believe me anyway," I groaned into the floorboards below.

"Why don't you try it," he said after a moment. "I like a good story as much as any."

I looked up into softer eyes. "We ran into a some Irish kids, and they took our..."

"Ah! Now *that* I might believe!" he interjected, sitting up and then leaning to look around at Isis. When he returned he said, "And who's goin'? Just you, or your friend here, too?"

" Both of us, sir. We have to."

"Have to," he said. "Both of you!" He drew a long breath. "All right. Five dollars eighty cents gets you a fare to Montreal. You double that and we're in business."

We were close, close enough, I hoped, and fished out our two coins up to nudge forward on the granite. "Sir. Can we get one ticket and work for the rest?"

He laughed. "Son, I can't help you with that."

I said we were good workers. And he could count on that, too!

"I don't doubt that my boy," he returned with an amused smile. "But I've got nothing for you here. You come up with eleven sixty, then we'll take care of you." He held up his newspaper to dismiss us. I stared at the masthead.

The Manchester Leader.
Saturday, August 8, 1863.

I pleaded we only need a little more! I said I had worked in a printing office once, and he snickered but said nothing, til I thanked him and turned away.

"And don't go begging around here," he called after. "I won't have none of that!"

I tried to remind myself that it was only what I'd expected, and that we'd have to go into the shops nearby and offer ourselves. Then, as it had earlier, Isis' step caught and I turned to see the last of a grimace.

"What's the matter?"

"Nothing," she said. "Only a little stomach is all."

But she took my suggestion that we sit for a while. We went to a dusky corner by the far end and sat back into one of the heavy benches. I told her she could wait here while I went after something. Maybe some work. No, she said; she'd only be a minute.

We settled back into the stillness, and after a minute or two I felt almost overwhelmingly tired.

But there was no relief. Scarcely another minute went by til I saw a fellow coming along at us briskly, as if at some purpose. A gentleman or a businessman of some sort, dressed in a frock coat and a black silk tie. On his head was a felt, fawn-colored bowler hat that he reached up to touch when he stopped a few feet away,.

"Afternoon, boys!" he said cheerfully. "You'll pardon me if I couldn't help noticing you having some difficulty back there."

"No trouble," I said. "We're just resting a bit."

"I thought you might be in need of something, some money perhaps."

Something kept me from blurting that we were.

"I could help, you see. I'm an artist. Harlon Peabody, you may have heard of me." He paused at my blank look. "I take photographic pictures, you see. Of prominent men and women, but - his eyes shifted to Isis - of other exceptional subjects now and then."

I looked at Isis. She glared. The man went on.

"I do have an eye for subjects, if I may say so, but let me come to the point. I can pay handsomely for an hour of your time."

"How much?" Isis snapped.

"Two dollars! How's that sound?"

"Ten!" she said.

He straightened back. Oh no, he couldn't manage *that*! Then a sly smile crept in. Like his! Croslin's! I sprang up.

"Keep it, mister. We don't want nothin' of yours!"

He shrank back, looked about, then touched at his hat. "As you wish, gentlemen," he said with a slight bow. I backed in to sit on the edge of the bench, watching him away til he faded beyond the near entry.

Isis slid over and nudged at my arm. She pointed toward a woman diagonally across the way—who was waving, and now dipping a finger several times in the direction of the ticket window. She called across. "I think he wants you."

"And who'd want to take a picture of you two?" said the agent, looking amused. He reached off his glasses, sighed, and sat back. "All right, I'll have the truth of this. You tell me what you're up to here and don't try to pull nothin'. I've seen many a young snap like you over the years."

"Montreal, sir. It's Montreal. We just have to get there and that's the truth!"

"And exactly why do you just *have* to?"

Once I began it came out like water over a falls. My brother at Gettysburg. Robert Smith and the letter and the woman and girl, the poem I found. "And my friend's had some trouble, too," I said.

I could see the agent's eyes change as he listened, and when I finished he looked at Isis. "Now tell me why you're here," he said.

"I'm going with Marty."

"I can see that, yes," he said, and waited.

"I can't tell you why."

"Can't. Can't tell me," he said. Their eyes held.

"All right. Then tell me this: are you a boy or a girl?"

Jeez! The silence swelled.

"I see," said the man quietly. "All right, now I *will* know this: This trouble you're in, is it with this boy here?"

She shook her head. "Marty's the only friend I got."

The agent nodded several times slowly, then looked off sideways. Then, abruptly, he reached in under the counter and brought out a small pad. "I'll need your names. First and last. And give me the spelling."

I could scarcely breathe - or didn't dare to for fear of dissolving our fortune.

He wrote carefully, then yanked the two sheets from the pad and thrust them out. "Take these," he said, "before I change my mind."

I thanked him like never anyone before while he looked back at me indulgently. "Comes time to board," he said, "you look for Mr. Russell, you won't miss him. You give him those," he said, pointing. "But mind you, they're good for today. Tonight. And that's all."

Yessirs! I gave him two or three, like gunshots.

"I want you on that platform at seven forty-five and not a minute before, is that clear?" And seconds later he called after. "Now get some shoes. And something to take with you to eat."

On Mr. Russell's head sat a dark blue box cap with a silver badge fixed in front. He wore no uniform but it was easy to be certain of him as we watched him bustle all about, tipping his cap, answering questions, now bending down to address a small child at a mother's side. He was slender, of medium height, and we liked him at once but held back to the last possible minute to reduce the chance of some reversal. (I have learned since that, while it didn't happen often, rail agents did have discretion to issue passes in circumstances they deemed worthy).

Neither of us had been on the cars before, nor had we, apart from newspaper illustrations, ever seen one of the big locomotives. Ned had once described them to me with typical embellishment: They were like black-plated giants breathing smoke and fire! And they were our own giants, with New Hampshire names out of lore.

Granite Maiden. Moosilauke. Chocorua.

A long whistle blew in the distance, and when a plume of smoke appeared and advanced over a row of low wooden buildings, we started forward.

And then it emerged, a ponderous beast, steaming and hissing and grinding, and squealing at last to a juddering halt that sent the four straw-yellow cars banging backwards into one another in succession, all the way to the almost toy-like red caboose at the end.

And here he was before us, all lettered out in foot-high gold along a deep green belly.

The Old Man of the Mountains.

We broke toward Mr. Russell, who'd headed up by boiler to look down the length of the train. We waited for him to turn, but he suddenly let go, long and loud.

"BOAR-R-RD! ALLL-LA-BOARRD!"

"Sir! - I all but shouted - Would you be Mr. Russell?"

He turned. "And I ain't hard of hearing. Not yet."

I apologized and held up the passes, which he took, but ignored while he looked me over. "Okay," he said. "I been expecting you." He looked at Isis, then back. "So . . . you talked old Patch Clifford into it, did you? Ain't easy to do that," he said. He looked down at the passes. Stroked at his chin. "What kind of name is this? Greek, is it?"

"It's Egyptian," said Isis, with a touch of pride. She'd always liked her name. The boys mocked it, but I never had, had never given in to that, at least.

"Egyptian! And what be you then, a princess?" he said with a gleam.

"I could be," she said a little teasingly, which broadened the man's smile. "Yes-s," he drawled, returning her spirit. "I think I see that."

He didn't linger, but directed us to the second car and said he'd check on us later, then stepped smartly away toward some others nearby.

. . .

A worn maroon carpet led down the center of the car. Perhaps half of the benches were occupied, but the wrought-iron racks above were mostly empty. We went to the front, where I stood aside for Isis to sit on the right by a window framed in dark green curtains. The glass needed cleaning, and the view for a short while, once we were underway, was further compromised by waves of engine smoke.

But then it was a marvel to see fence posts and fields sweep past at an astonishing clip, houses and barns, pastures studded with cows, occasionally a wooded interlude.

And here came a boy, waving and waving - and gone, along with the dog barking at his side. The car jiggered along, and the rattling from below made it a challenge to speak, even if we weren't much inclined to it.

It might have been a half an hour til exhaustion caught us both up and slid us both down into the bench to gaze weakly ahead. I tried to identify a pervasive, though not unpleasant odor (coal oil, I learned later). The evening light faded and after our second stop, in Tilton, Mr. Russell came by to light the lanterns at the ends of the car. I wasn't surprised to see Isis with even less left in her than me. I dozed here and there, but she slept, even through one stop altogether. And once I thought I saw pain in her face when she shifted.

The lamplight from a few feet ahead glowed, honey-like, and I kept thinking of Mama and how she herself might by now have raised a lamp in the parlor. I wondered if it would be like it had been before when she'd sat up nights after we'd learned about Ned. And Father! He'd be home from Keene now, or Brattleboro! And I thought how Mama had probably been left to all the milking on her own!

And hadn't Isis known all this! Hadn't she tried to tell me!

. . .

Sometime later there came a tug at my shoulder, then another. "Son? I'm gonna need you a minute."

I'd been asleep on my side and rose awkwardly, blinking into a spray of sparks flying past outside. Mr. Russell told me were coming into Woodsville, where we'd be staying a while to take on wood before crossing the river into Vermont. His next words gave me a start. "I'll be finishing up here," he said, "but you'll be fine. Mr. Jeannotte will have your passes and be with you the rest of the way." Only after he left did I look down and see that I'd been lying on a small round cushion.

Isis was asleep on a cushion of her own. But the hat had slipped to the floor, and her exposed head brought me an instant of alarm. And all at once I saw her holding an ax above a hairy face - and realized I had dreamed of it some time before.

I decided not to rouse her and stepped down from the car to be hailed by a group of men who'd been recruited to load and bring wheelbarrows of cordwood to the tender from a nearby shed. I took the gloves offered me but declined a leather jacket. And each time I returned, I glanced up hoping to see Isis on the platform, or at least watching in the window.

I bought four hard-boiled eggs and some biscuits from a woman, then re-boarded to find Isis sitting up. She wasn't hungry, she said, and shook her head when I asked once more if she was okay.

THIRTEEN

I wakened to flashes of sunlight in the window—and to an ache still at my ankle. She was already up and sitting on the bench ahead with her back against the window; a blanket had been folded and hung over the seatback between us. She was just finishing an egg.

"We're in United Canada," she said. "That's what the man called it ⋯ and you can sure tell he's French! He left us some water," she said and pointed at a tin cup and a small jug. I gazed at her in relief. She'd recovered. She even looked cheery.

But Canada. I had expected a thoroughly wooded landscape, like something from the pages of *The Deerslayer*, yet here all was open, unrelentingly flat farmland. And the houses: Here came one - and the small barn beside - both painted in bright sky-blue! Then others flew by, humble clapboard farmhouses like ours at home, but also starkly different: an added pitch or curve in the roof, a steeper angle; and whole dwellings set in the open in pastel pink or green!

I sat back in wonder. For here it was yet again.

The same, but different!

Or was it the other way round?

Then from out of the blue came this.

"You've been a good friend, Marty," she said musingly, not looking at me, but ahead. "You didn't go along. Anyhow, not mostly."

What was this?

The car swung outward, pulling our weight.

"Not that one time though. At my desk," she resumed when the car straightened. She looked back at me with a smile. "I remember that."

Oh, hadn't we both! A touch of the old sting bit in me, but it was easy to tell her I felt bad about it, even right away afterward. She did, too, she said.

It was five or six years ago. Scoonie Fenn had been giving me the old business about Isis: friends with an Indian, friends with a girl; and at my denial snarling, "Prove it, Dascomb!"

I tried. I went up by her bench, not knowing what I'd do. She was at work on a pencil drawing of a horse. "That ain't no good!" I said and snatched at the page, turned and held it out toward Scoonie. "Lookit this." And then for all the world to see I held it high and tore it down the middle.

She was already out of her seat when I turned back, and the sound of my cheek surely reached all four walls, and then she went straight past to Scoonie and hard-smacked him the same.

But that wasn't all. Later Scoonie waited for me at the bottom of the hill and sent me home with a bloody lip. And this second humiliation was followed by a third at home when Ned told me I'd gotten just what I deserved.

"Don't you ever let Scoonie Fenn decide your friends for you," he said.

I asked what brought this up now. She didn't answer and instead told me she was sorry for that other time, too. I looked at her for a moment - and then blushed.

"Oh jeez, *that*!" I said. I said I didn't know why I'd done it! We'd neither of us brought it up since then. Two years and it was still just as confusing, painful, shameful, degrading.

"You're a boy is all," she shrugged. "I shouldn't ⋯ and what I said, I didn't mean it."

I told her I knew. And I did. More than ever I did! "Anyway," I said, "it don't matter now."

Mr. Jeannotte spread his legs for balance and with a hand steadied himself on the seatback. He was a middle-aged, square-headed fellow, dressed in a gold-buttoned, blue uniform jacket and matching box-cap. He began in a heavily accented voice that took some concentration to follow. He wanted us to know about the Saint Lawrence River coming up and what we'd need to be ready for in the crossing. But then he shifted and told us how he'd been on this line between 'Moh-rayall' and Woodsville for the whole ten years of its operation. He said, it hadn't run in the winter months when ice had all but cut his city off for several months of the year - not until four years ago when the new bridge had opened.

"Veectoria!" he said proudly. "Eez longest breege in ze world! Tree kilometers," he said and thought. "Two miles, yes?" he asked, nodding. Then he cupped his ears and grinned. "But ze noize! Not zo bad, I tink. But ze firz time!" He winced, then told us that the Victoria was a long, iron-plated tube set on stone pillars high above the river. And the only opening, he said, as he tipped his head back to look up at the ceiling. He raised his hands for a second and held them a foot apart. "Zo much only," he said. "For ze smoke, ze gas." And we'd spend a full six minutes in total darkness.

"Zo!" he said finally. "What you tink, now you know!"

We were glad he'd warned us and thanked him. But all throughout, half my mind had been occupied with questions. I started with how big the city was.

"Eez beeg, ey. One hundre-towzen!"

I sagged at the unimaginable number, but he went proudly on and said Montreal was the tenth largest city in North America, Half French, half English. And its name came from a mountain "right in ze middle."

I asked if he knew of any Negroes - and repeated it at his widened eyes. "Negroes. Colored people," I said. "Are there many there?" But still, in mild confusion he only looked down at me.

And then I went right to it. I told him that my brother had been killed in the war and that there was a woman we had to find, a Negro who knew something about him. "We have to find her, sir. Can you help us any?"

"Zees war! Oui!" he said, looking a little pinched. "Eez terrible ting. Even we 'ave some here joined."

"Yes, sir," I said. "But are there any, any Negroes?"

"Here? Two, tree hundred only," he said and held up a thumb and forefinger together. "Uh soupçon, ey!" He paused and smiled. "Only leetle pepper in zee deesh."

"Do you know where any live?" I asked, sitting in.

"One. 'Ee 'ave a barbershop."

I sat up. "Where? Where is that?"

He said it was down by the river, by the shipping wharfs. He said a fellow had a shop where the English gentlemen went. Businessmen. He gave us a name. I asked him to write it out and he did, on the back of my pass before handing it out to me. Shadrach Minkins, it said.

We were ready for the passage. Or thought we were. The train slowed. Then came a rumbling in the car ahead, followed quickly by a burst of sound that sent my hands to my ears. Isis threw her arms about her tummy and hunched forward. I reached out a hand to her shoulder.

I may have said something, but it was useless to speak.

In the station, when we stood to go, she winced and briefly clutched at herself. And yet again she shook me off, saying girls had cramps like these sometimes. I didn't believe it and now, for the first time, I understood that something was truly the matter. I watched her ahead for a few steps, til she turned and waved me on.

The Bonaventure Station was a lofty and unimaginably ornate great hall; you might have set two barns like ours at home in it end to end. Outside, I looked up to see three towers above the station, each topped by a massive flag; I recognized the French and English, but the third, in blue with a white cross, I'd never seen.

It was midmorning now as we made began our way down Prince Street. Four and five-story, brownstone buildings lined both sides of the busy thoroughfare, all the way down to the rippling river below and the far shore beyond. Men in suits hustled along in both directions on cobblestone walks still damp from an earlier shower, but the air had brightened.

The view opened wide at the bottom, and now the river looked more like a sea. It was filled with small boats. Several larger ones moved slowly under sail. The current gleamed. We stood mesmerized for a minute before I stepped out to look upriver and find a cluster of tall masts behind a long grey-stone building. Was that our shipyard? My heart bumped and then sank at thought of yet another beginning.

It wasn't long til we found it, a weathered, stoic post with faded stripes that had surely endured many a winter. And behind it a slender redbrick building with a half-sized door and a small window to one side. And a sign. We advanced.

Shaving and Hair Cutting Emporium.

"Must be fancy," she said. "What's that mean, Em ... Emporium." I told her in haste and went to the door, where an oval brass plate in the center proclaimed we'd arrived at *77 1/2*!

At another time I would have laughed. But a smaller shop raised our chances of finding the man alone, or perhaps with only one. I glanced up the street and down and saw no one coming along.

Two faces lifted as I stood in the entry; the third, standing, turned to me from his work. He was a slightly built but handsome brown-faced man of advanced years, with a high forehead and wiry, short-cropped silvery hair. No one spoke.

It was a small room cramped with chairs and stands and a high, black-lacquered sideboard that took up most of the back wall, though a large mirror above returned some sense of space and depth. I drew myself up.

"Begging your pardon, sir," I began. "We've been sent here to find Mr. Minkins."

"Shad? What you got with Shad?" the barber asked in a rich, baritone voice.

I told him we needed help finding someone.

"Ain't lookin' for nothin'," he scoffed. "Belong in school that's what."

I began again but his eye cut to Isis. "Nobody teach you 'bout dat hat?" he demanded.

Isis hesitated, then reached up slowly, and when her head was bared, the two others broke grins. "There you go, Shad," sneered one. "You teach 'em if the nuns up there can't."

"He doesn't need a haircut!" quipped the other.

"I'm sorry, sir, but .."

"Ain't no sorries in here, boy!" said the barber, waving me off.

"No, sir. But just now we came from New Hampshire and we gotta find someone."

His head tilted. "What you got wif New Ham'sher? Nobody sent you fum New Ham'sher!"

"Honest. We did! Just now! On the train!"

He thought a moment. "I know 'bout New Ham'sher," he said. "What you got wif dat?

I glanced at the others, one then the other, and then all but erupted into my story; and at a pace and a voice that hardly allowed interruption.

Five or ten minutes later Mr. Minkins stood outside with us on the stoop, having given us directions to a dwelling owned by a Mr. George Drummond. After telling us he came down the first of every month. After telling us he was "the finest gen'man. And after telling us that, indeed, the woman, Marie, lived up there with her child! He and his wife had brought her back. On a ship. Before the war.

All of that had I heard, almost breathlessly.

And how had the mention of New Hampshire turned our fortune? We learned that years earlier a U.S. senator from New Hampshire, a Mr. Hale, had been a major factor in Shadrach Minkins' life after he'd escaped from slavery, first to Boston and then on to New Hampshire, where Mr. Hale took him on and later helped establish him in Montreal.

I looked again at the rough, blocky script penciled onto the slip of paper in my hand.

DRUMMIN. MONTIN STREET.
CURTSEY OF SHADRACH MINKINS.

We paused for a last look out over the water before turning back up into the city, where everything now would be a climb. Isis kept a slow but steady pace, and whatever discomfort she yet suffered she bore well. I still had hopes that it might pass. Or had.

New preoccupations arose: What would the woman say? What would she look like, what would she do?

Hello, I'm Ned Dascomb's brother. We got a letter at home and I . . .

We made our way past row upon row of brick and stone buildings, past the strong smell of frying onions, by people speaking streams of French while gesturing with their hands. And always the relentless uphill slope.

But the sun's heat began to wear on Isis, and in the middle of a square, where children were at play on the steps below a stone obelisk, I turned to see her shouldered against a lamppost.

"What is it?" I said. She looked back blankly. "WHAT?" I cried and threw looks about. An elderly woman stopped to ask something in French. I looked at her, then at Isis, who only closed her eyes and looked aside. I looked back at the woman. She shrugged and moved on. I took Isis by the hand and led her to a nearby bench. I said we must be close by now. I told her to rest here and I'd get help. "No," she said. "Just a few minutes."

A passersby confirmed that Sherbrooke and then our turn from it was only just ahead.

She held out her hands for me to bring her up, and we went on with my arm hooked through one of hers, and for a short while with a hand on her shoulder.

And finally we were there—before an arched iron gate, beyond which stood an enormous gray stone house!

And here Isis collapsed.

FOURTEEN

I heard her yawp after I'd let go her arm and advanced a step or two, gazing in disbelief at such a house as this before us. She had sunk against one of the stone pillars. There was a blot between her legs, a dark patch the size of a saucer! Her eyes had withdrawn.

I stood over her, staring down. I lurched and spun half way round, then back again and froze.

My chest swelled tight. My forehead throbbed. And all at once I jerked at the front of my shirt, tore it open, then yanked it free and began twisting it about my hand. I dropped to a knee. One arm went behind and with the other, with my fist, I pressed at her there. I said some things, I didn't know what. I'd been entirely taken over and was no longer Martin William Dascomb.

And what I remember most: She was like clay. Both the look and the soft, lifeless impression of her.

"Can you hold this?" I breathed into her ear. "Can you? I gotta go to the house." Her hand moved slowly and settled over mine. "I'll only be a minute," I whispered. "Only a minute and I'll be back."

I vaulted a low iron fence and kept on at a sprint. I saw a man kneeling in a bed of flowers by the house, stopped and hollered, waved and went on. He came out of the garden and threw up an arm.

"Arête! Arête!"

I kept on.

"Arête! Regardez!" he demanded, jabbing at me repeatedly with the trowel in his hand.

"I need help!" I cried when I stood panting five feet away. "Get help! Please! Please, my friend!" He glared at me a moment, then pointed the trowel at my feet.

"*Ici! Ici!*"

I nodded and nodded and squeezed my eyes shut.

He waited til my quieter look assured him, then turned off toward a nearby side door, where he turned and pointed once more at my feet.

A man in a black suit and bow tie emerged to address me in a voice full of calm authority. "Please explain this intrusion, young man!"

I pointed toward the gate and pleaded that my friend was bleeding over there. He held my eyes. Then he turned and spoke to the gardener in French.

"Wait here," he said to me.

He left and shortly after a young woman came out and said simply, "Where?"

She moved along briskly before me, and when her pace quickened, I took an eager hop to keep up.

Isis's eyes were half open, but weak. The woman knelt and gently lifted her hand, then the shirt.

"What is her name?" she asked over her shoulder, and when I told her, it seemed her head gave a little start. She turned. "All right, you run back and tell them I need Flora. Flora," she repeated. "Tell them I need two linens, anything that's handy, and some water in a jug. And a glass. Can you remember all that?"

"Linens, some water," I said.

And a glass," she said. "And Flora!"

• • •

The side of the house was like a high looming wall, and I sat below it for a time with my knees drawn up in my arms, then I paced up and down the cobblestones. It felt like an hour before the door finally opened to a third woman who, like Flora, was dressed in a servant's black and white. Over her arm was another linen, which gave me an acute start when she held it out. *A shirt!* All my scrawny self had been exposed this whole while!

She beckoned me in and I followed her down a narrow corridor into a small, spare room holding two chairs and a modest wooden desk. The maid hadn't spoken and didn't now. She pointed me to sit and quietly left, but it was only minute or two til I heard footsteps return. I watched the doorknob turn, and looked up into the solemn face of the tall, slender young woman in green who had attended to Isis and ordered her brought in. I stood but she motioned me down. "We've sent for the doctor," she said and went round to sit herself at the desk. She leaned in. "I need to know where she lives. And her name, her full name."

I told her. "But she doesn't live here," I said. "We both came just this morning on the cars, from New Hampshire." Her eyes widened, and she looked away for a time.

Her face was long and lean, but her nose was broad and had already appeared somewhat out of keeping; and spreading over it from cheek to cheek I'd seen a spray of freckles. Her dark, coppery hair had earlier been tied in a bandana, but now it hung loosely about her shoulders. And I'd never seen the like of her eyes: They were green, with flecks of yellowish grey.

It was a minute before she turned back.

"Your friend is seriously ill," she said. "And you're telling me you came from New Hampshire; we don't have time for foolishness."

I said it was true and hung my head.

I heard her sigh of displeasure. "And just what are you doing here," she said, "from New Hampshire?"

"We came to find someone," I said meekly.

"And you brought your friend here in *that* condition?"

I groaned and my voice pitched up as I said I didn't know. I stared at my trembling hands.

"She's a friend. Not your sister."

I shook my head.

"What's her age, how old is she?"

"Almost fourteen," I said. "Same as me."

"Fourteen!" she said and leaned in hard. "Now. Tell me. Are you responsible for the state she's in?"

"No-O! It was only a stomach. Some cramps, she said."

She sat back, heaved a deep sigh, and her next words struck me like an iron bar.

"Your friend was carrying a child," she said. "You didn't know that?"

. . .

I opened my eyes to a planked wall twelve inches away. And again came the strange-sounding words that had wakened me.

Reveillez-vous. Reveillez!

I had spent the night in the carriage house on a cot in a narrow room above the horses. I followed my old friend, the gardener, down the staircase and past as fine a pair of Morgans as ever I'd set eyes upon. Outside I looked up at the two massive chimneys. He led me into the house and along a hallway filled with the smell of baking bread and left me in a plain, yellow-walled room containing an eight-foot dining table and a number of surrounding simple chairs. A few minutes later a bosomy woman bustled in carrying a breakfast tray. She smiled me a short greeting in French, set the tray down before me and withdrew. Ten minutes later, dressed in deep blue, the young woman, my inquisitor, came in to greet and sit opposite me. She set a pencil and pad down between us and asked if I'd had enough to eat; she said there'd be more if I wanted.

"We need to send a wire to her parents. And one to yours." Then she held my eyes. "But I haven't asked your name, have I?" She raised her chin and something in her smile chilled me as she peered across.

"I'm wondering if you're a Dascomb," she said. She paused. "Martin, if I have it right."

The shock in my face affirmed it.

The smile deepened. She leaned in and slid a hand out across the table.

"Let me tell you mine," she said. "I am Marie."

I sat, blank-faced.

"Let me tell you about your friend," she said. "Then we'll take a walk."

She said Isis was sleeping and wouldn't be left alone. The doctor had been in. Childbed Fever, was what he'd called it.

I blundered to my feet and followed her along out into the air and light.

She had known my name!

The garden behind the house was like a sea of flowers with its surface all afloat in rows of reds and yellows, lavender; white, orange and blue. It was framed behind and along two sides by a brick wall nearly my height. She paused in the main entry before white-pebbled paths leading left and right as well as a wider one down the center. We turned right til we came to a small, circular pool, where she beckoned me to sit on a stone bench in the shade of a tree hung with clutches of orange berries. We'd been silent til now.

She looked out. "So. You've met my friend Robert I take it. Or someone has."

I said it was me. I told her how he'd found me and left the letter. I waited for another question. And I puzzled. Was this she? A Negro? Why had she written that? *Had* she written that?

"And Ned," she said. "He'd be off in the army, I suppose."

"Ned?" I said, and repeated it, hearing my voice rise and twist around the image of him. "Ned?"

"Is he in the army?"

My eyes watered full and I sat. I sat.

And she waited in the stillness - til I felt her touch on my arm.

I looked up into glistening eyes, a serene smile.

"When?" she said. "When was it?"

I told her, looking down into her folded hands. I told her where and how, and then she reached to cover my hand. And after a minute she said he'd be proud of me for coming.

We sat for a time in the stillness and all the bright color before us before she said she'd like to hear what had brought me all this way. Just now and with her, with Isis.

I told her about the letter and Mama and how later I'd heard her at a lullaby and seen changes in her. I told her about Isis coming to the house with the bruise and how we both needed to *do something*! It wasn't long, and I didn't mention the suspicions of her being a Negro.

"Well," she said and rose to look down at me. "I think it's time you met Sophie."

In the pool ahead, a foot or two beyond its stone border, I saw a lazy roll of orange just under the surface. I took a step in to watch as the tail feathered up and then slipped away into the dark. The impression lingered as we walked away, and I allowed the wonder of a kind of witness having been among us.

"Your voice is a little like his, you know," she said. "I can't put my finger on it, but something in it gave me the first thought of who you might be." She turned me an easy smile and added that she thought she'd seen one or two other resemblances, too, but she left these unspoken.

Toward the far end of the garden we came into a large semicircle with marble benches all along the outer edge. Yet another marvel! Like a small amphitheater! We turned through it and into the wider path leading back through the center. The great stone house and its chimneys loomed beyond. She stopped by a sundial on a granite pedestal and turned.

"Martin. As soon as I can arrange it, we must send you home; your mother will be beside herself."

I stared.

"Oh surely you must know this!" she said.

• • •

I waited outside til I heard steps behind the door, then a high-pitched voice. And then in the threshold, dressed in full-skirted, sky blue and clutching a doll to her breast, stood a little being with a stern face. Her hair was tied back, but even at first glance I saw that it was his. Thin, straight, the same dull grayish-gold. She looked down at me, full of suspicion.

"This is Martin, Sophie. He's been waiting to meet you."

Her head tipped a little and her pale eyes held me, much as a superior might.

"Martin has come a long way," said Marie.

"Why?" came the little voice.

"We'll never mind that just now. And you might say hello!"

"Anyway, I saw you awready!"

"You did?" I said, warming, all wide-eyed.

"Uh-huh. Before. When you were sad I was yooking out the window."

"You were?"

"Your face was dirty, too," she said. "Were you crying?"

"Sophie!" said Marie, turning on her. I began to protest, with a smile broken out full, but Sophie cut me short.

"Cuz your friend was sick, that's why," she said.

I laughed, wondrously and quite out loud and it felt a sudden miracle that such a thing was still in me.

And now, slowly, one side of the little mouth curled up.

Exactly like his!

FIFTEEN

After Marie went off to the city in a carriage, I was moved into the big house. A maid led me up the servant staircase to the third floor and along a corridor to a small, white-walled room toward the front of the house. Beyond the iron bedstead a window looked out onto the side yard; and to one side I caught sight of the gate and pillar where Isis had given out. I felt ponderously heavy and lay down. But my head, full of images and fearful thoughts, gave me no peace.

I took my dinner as before, alone in the servants' room. Marie came in toward the end to let me know that Isis' fever remained stable, though they were watching her closely. Isis had taken some broth, but mostly she slept. I had no mood for it, but agreed when Marie offered to bring me something to read. She asked what I liked, and I shrugged but told her I'd been reading Dickens at home.

"Well," she said with a smile and a cock of her head. "I would have thought that a little bleak for us just now."

She led me up the narrow staircase and all the way to my door, where she handed me the books she'd brought up under an arm. One was a favorite of Mr. Drummond, she said, a book of poems by a Scottish writer. It was the first mention of the master of the house, and she went on to say that he'd been away at his business for a week but was expected back anytime, perhaps tomorrow. "Perhaps you might meet him," she said, and withdrew after reminding me that it wouldn't do to go in to Isis, who as I knew was at the other end of the hall behind the first door!

She'd also given me a new and better fitting shirt she'd gotten in town. I set it aside and went back to sit on the edge of the bed. *Walden*. I hadn't read it, but it had been a favorite of Ned's. I wondered if she had known that.

The Pilgrim's Progress. This one I had attempted two years ago at Father's urging. I'd found it tedious, though Ned had told me I'd find more in it if I waited a few years. I turned inside to the title page.

THE PILGRIM'S PROGESS FROM THIS WORLD TO THAT WHICH IS TO COME DELIVERED UNDER THE SIMILITUDE OF A DREAM

"Hah!" I said aloud and snapped the cover shut.

The last was bound in green leather with gold lettering. *Poems by Robert Burns*. I opened to a page in the middle and tried a few lines. Then went to another page. And another. Half the words looked like English, the rest partly something else. I groaned and slapped the covers shut.

My dreams were a shifting spectacle of faces and voices. But even now, after all these years, the remains of one stays with me. I am sitting with Marie in the garden by a pool. I am struggling to convince her of something, but my mouth is like the mouth a fish; it opens and closes and nothing comes out. I am underwater and at the bottom, in the mud far below, I see two small fire-orange orbs shimmering like miniature suns. My need for them is overwhelming, and I am a sudden fury of arms and legs. Down and down and down I struggle, but not ⋯ not getting… And my chest! My lungs!

Perhaps I should not admit to the recurrence of this nightmare more than once in the years since, though in somewhat different forms and never quite so wildly, but with the same or similar spheres. They seem to exist like an unfinished painting on a wall in some dark corridor of my memory.

Marie awakened me in the morning with a light rapping at the door. "It's eight o'clock," she said and waited til she heard me rouse. "It's nothing to be alarmed about, but I need you downstairs."

What she needed me for were measurements! For a suit of clothes! She wanted me going home looking proper. And also, if I didn't object, she wanted a photograph taken of me with Sophie—and including her, too, if it seemed appropriate. She wanted something for Sophie. And for me, if I liked, to take home.

I asked when, when would I go back?

"Soon enough," she said. "When you're rested,"

With the butler's assistance, Marie took lengths, turning me awkwardly this way and that, much to the amusement of Sophie standing by. She'd said there was a clothier in town who could have something altered on short notice. "You'll be something to see, your mother will think so," she said.

It was an ordeal, but came with a benefit. As I stood there, self-conscious and obedient, I think Sophie saw me just as how I felt myself: like something of a mannequin, a doll. I sensed it bringing me sympathy and even a touch of affection. In any event, Sophie was eager for it when sometime after she was given the chance to spend time with me outside,

She came down with her hair in ribbons and a pinafore tied over a gray-spotted maroon dress. She took my hand to cross the cobbled drive and with the other pointed at the wide carriage house entry. "I can't go in there," she said. "But sometimes I do with *Mamá!*"

We stopped under one of the maples by the drive. Some of the lawn was in shade but most of it gleamed bright in the sun. Not ideal for hide-and-seek, I thought. But for her, safe. She threw up her hands at my suggestion.

"Goody! I know that!" She looked out and pointed to a cluster of shrubs. "I'm gonna hide over *there*!"

"No-no-no!" I grinned. "Don't tell! First I have to blind my eyes and count, and *then* you hide."

She looked up at me, glaring. "I *want* to hide there!"

"But then I'll know already, won't I?"

She thought. "Way'oo, go somewhere else!" she said and gave me a sour face when I laughed.

She also didn't understand about staying hidden, or so I thought at the time. I was yards away and finished my slow count with an emphatic "TEN!" But when I announced I was coming and stepped out from behind the tree, she popped up full of glee.

"Here I'yam!"

Again, I explained. She giggled, nervously, and looked away; she wasn't confident of me, not yet. I took another proper hide of my own and then tried again, pitching my voice up theatrically.

"Won't this be fun THIS TIME," I said. "Looking for Sophie while she stays still; maybe she will this time!"

She didn't.

I stood with fists held exaggeratedly at my hips and fibbed. "Okay, you did a little better this time."

We were better at tag, and it took only a few minutes to lose ourselves in giggling dodges and sweeping hands, shrieks and whirls and wide-faced pauses for breath. And when at last it felt like enough, I fled away into the shade and fell back, face up and spread-eagle. And I remember it now, how my chest heaved and heaved and then quieted under all the green melting over me from above, how I'd returned for a time to who I once was. Sophie stood by, looking down at me til I sat up.

"I forgot your name," she said. And then, "No, your *yast* name!"

She took me round to her sandbox by the side of the carriage house, and for a while, with bits of this and that, we made and decorated cakes. Then we shaped up a house, completing it with a twig she snapped in two to put a chimney at each end. "I yike fires when it's cohd," she said.

When we finished and went out toward the house, I looked up at the half open window of Isis' room on the third floor.

After lunch Marie put me at work helping the gardener, who, with his slouch hat pulled low, spoke little and all of it in French. He led me out back into the deep beds, where I spent an hour deadheading dahlias and tall hollyhocks. I went back to him, but he didn't employ me further, and for a while I only sat nearby in silence. Marie came up to my room later to say that the lady of the house had invited the two of us to sit with her for a four o'clock tea!

I washed and tidied up, yet felt myself still a hapless rustic as I trailed Marie out, for the first time, into the interior of the main floor - where I found myself once again in the pages of *Harper's Weekly*. Gilt-framed oil portraits hung between high oaken doors on the left; on the right a six-inch, carved bannister rose alongside an eight-foot-wide staircase. Ahead was a high circular entry with a chandelier the size of a washtub hanging in the middle.

Marie hooked my arm and turned to face us through a ten-foot entry into a deep room. An astonishingly young woman sat alone in the center of the room. I swept my eyes about for someone else.

"Let's meet Mrs. Drummond, shall we?" said Marie, but then feeling only my weight, she turned to me with an amused smile. "Oh goodness, I should have prepared you. I *am* sorry."

Couches, chairs and tables were clustered together in groups. A grand piano stood at the far end, with a marble bust on a pedestal beside. Two long tapestries hung on the inner wall, though the light from the windows on the left hardly reached them.

The woman rose from her loveseat and began toward us. She was slight of figure, with a pale, triangular face and flaxen hair braided up behind her ears. I took my eyes away when it was clear she was headed directly at me.

She took up my hands and said she was pleased to meet me, but wished these terrible circumstances might have been different. Then her grip firmed.

"I don't expect you to say anything," she said. "In fact, I don't want you to. But I want you to know this, that I never had the chance to meet your brother and I very much wish that I had." Then she raised our hands between us and leaned back. "But I have met you, haven't I?" she said with a warm smile.

She beckoned us in. Marie and I took the two upholstered chairs facing her across a mahogany table with an elaborately carved border. The lady reached for a tiny silver bell and gave it a few short shakes before settling back. There'd be tea, and scones, she said and then to me, "and ginger ale, too. It's something a little different, perhaps you'll try it."

She said was pleased that I'd met Sophie and hoped I didn't mind that she'd watched us at play for a while, that it was always a delight to see her outside like that with others. "You were *very* good with her," she said and then sat forward. "I'll take just a minute about your friend," she said and smiled. "Your friend with the unusual name."

I said it was an Egyptian name - the first words I'd spoken. "But she isn't that," I said. She didn't take it up but went on to how to assure me they were doing everything possible and that their doctor was the very best. I nodded back several times.

"Now, if I were you," she said a little playfully after settling back, "I think I would have questions about us here."

I had none, none I dared voice. "No Ma'am," I said.

"Oh?" said Marie with a glint in her eye.

"Well, let me tell you that Mr. Drummond is away," said the lady before turning to Marie. "But we expect him the day after tomorrow, will it be possible to meet him?"

"I don't know that," Marie returned. "It's possible; we'll have to see."

The lady said that her husband was a sugar merchant, as his father had been before him, and that the family had done business for many years in New Orleans. "Ah, maybe you know of it!" she said when I looked up, already sensing where we might be headed.

She said they still had many friends there and that some of them, whole families, used to come up to Montreal in the summer months to escape the heat and mosquitoes. "But that was some time ago, before this war. And I should tell you that New Orleans was once a *very* special place; it was home to many different kinds of people,"

I drew a breath, felt the beating of my heart.

But just then came a rattling from behind us beyond the entry. The lady looked up and gave a little clap.

A maid pushing a tea wagon came in to stop and fill two teacups, then take up one of two bottles from which she poured a tumbler of something clear and bubbly. She stepped back and gave a little bow.

"Thank you, Margaret. And thank you for remembering the sarsaparilla, too" the lady said, and then to me: "In case what I hope you will try isn't to your taste."

I said no, I hadn't heard of ginger ale. She told me it was popular in the cities just now and had come from Ireland, had originated there, she thought. She waited while I sipped at something both peppery and sweet; and when I said I liked it she pointed to a small covered dish. There were ice chips if I wanted.

And now she returned to New Orleans. She said that for more than two centuries the city had brought people together from many different races and nationalities: French, English, Spanish, African Negroes and American Indians. And for generations all these had lived and worked together in harmony. Many had intermarried.

I felt the moment gathering.

"And the children of these mixed-race unions," she went on, "these came to have a special name."

I looked off into the tapestry on the wall, at a dim, forested scene full of animals.

"In English we say they are People of Color."

To one side a stag on the run.

"In French the term is *gens de couleur*," she said.

I held my eyes away.

"I am one," said Marie quietly behind me. "I am one, myself. A person of color."

For a moment it baffled me. But hadn't I had known something like this all along? Seen but not allowed the pieces to fit? Her words in the letter and then the extraordinary, never before red-gold of her face and all along her arms? My forehead throbbed.

"It's not easy to accept, I know that," Marie said, and then after a moment, "Look at me."

The soft smile matched the sound of her voice. And then it *did* feel easier; it felt like something in me had simply let go and faded.

Wouldn't I take a scone, Mrs. Drummond asked. They'd been fresh-baked that morning. And the apple and pear jam was of their own making.

A few minutes later Marie began to tell of her background. She had a great-grandmother who'd been from Africa and later had a child by her white slave owner. She said there were no records and she had no idea who the man was. And now, three generations later, she herself was of mostly French and Scottish blood, but was still referred to as an Octoroon. She asked if I'd heard of the term and I told her I'd read *Uncle Tom's Cabin*, which brought exclamations from them both.

Her father was a successful clothier with a shop of his own, and there were many of African heritage like them; they were just another part of New Orleans society. But then the threat of abolitionism grew, and grew, and the city lost its tolerance. Restrictive laws were passed that put anyone of Negro ancestry, no matter how distant the blood lines, at risk of expulsion or enslavement. And all of this was based in something called the 'one-drop rule'.

"One drop!" said Marie. "Of what! Of blood! Can you imagine it?" she said. "Your brother's child taken as property?" She looked off.

"That was two years ago," said the lady a few moments after. She said that after Mr. Lincoln had been elected she and her husband decided to go down and bring them out. She told me she was two years older than Marie but that they'd been friends since they were young girls. And then came this, that made saucers of my eyes.

"But we are sisters now," she said. "My brother and her sister were married, what, almost a decade ago."

One, then the other, sipped at tea.

"So you see, it's a wide world. Or it was," Marie took up. "And your brother, you know he…"

But she faltered. She brought the cup up, and held it, then lowered it again and shifted away. She sighed. "We've all paid a price, haven't we. But you more than most." Then her voice drifted as she sat looking out a window, her two hands cradling the cup in her lap. "Your brother wanted to be a part of something, you know." She reached up to rub at an eye. Mrs. Drummond sat out toward her, but Marie straightened and turned back. "I think it's time I told you about us," she said.

They had met at a dinner party, at the home of Henry Rutherford, Ned's college friend, with whom he'd been staying. It was a formal evening with some twenty guests, and at the last minute Marie had been called in to help serve. And very soon, she said, she had begun to feel Ned's eyes following her about the long table. She was embarrassed at first, and then grew perturbed. "I'm sure you know your brother hadn't much use for liquor," she said, "but I think the men had gotten to him a little beforehand; that's how I explain it. Anyway, after a while I came around behind to take up a plate, and he looked up at me, right in the eye. He didn't say anything but his eyes were ···" She smiled. "Well, didn't I gave him a glare! And after that he disguised himself. Some. But I still felt his eyes."

She paused for a sip and continued. "He came to the house the next day and asked to speak with my father. And they talked. For an hour, or Ned did, as I heard. He told my father he'd gone off to college to be a minister but changed his mind and intended to study the law. He wanted to work toward some new ways." She leaned in to set the cup and saucer on the table. "Wouldn't you know, my father took to him. He gave his permission to see me if I wanted, which decidedly I did not!" She was smiling now, almost enjoying this "He wrote me," she said. "And I wrote back. I refused him, and then he had Henry come by on his behalf."

She turned to face me more directly. "I was only *seventeen*! Still young!" she said as a twinkle came into her eye. "But I think it's fair to say ··· that in some ways your brother wasn't any older, or wiser."

She cast a questioning glance at Mrs. Drummond, who raised a hand at once. "Oh goodness no, I shan't mind this again."

Ned had come to dinner with her family, then they began seeing each other. He came by every day, sometimes twice. They went for walks and drives, and talked for hours. Ned told her about us at home. "And oh yes, about your father," she said. She brushed at her hair. "I heard all about their troubles; it was a heavy burden on him, I suppose you know that."

Her expression changed when she said that talk of Ned had begun. "It wasn't seeing me," she said, "so much as it was his teaching at night. He'd go off evenings to meet a group of Negroes in their church, I suppose you know that. Robert was among them."

Her voice darkened after a pause.

"I tried. Henry did, and some others, too. But none of us …" She broke off and leaned in for the cup and saucer, but then left it to straighten and look out past the lady.

"He was so stubborn, when all that might have been avoided," she said wistfully. "Henry took the blame on himself, but the two of them, they were just two Yankee graduates filled with grand ideas. And sometimes I think Ned *wanted* to make the water boil."

She turned back to me. Then her eyes opened wide.

"Oh surely he told you! Martin!"

"He wouldn't."

But your parents!"

I shook my head. "He wouldn't talk of it."

"None of you?" she said.

I blinked at the sting in my eyes. I told her all Father said was that he'd been run out.

She reached out to cover my hand. "It might have been worse," she said. "He might have been beaten; it was only because Henry's family were so prominent." Her hand slipped away. "He didn't tell you any of this?"

Then she told me the end of it. Henry had come around in a state one morning and told her four men had gone to the church the night before and taken Ned off. One went to Henry, and Henry warned them, had them promise not to harm him.

She said she had waited for Ned to write and was surprised at first when he didn't. She said she had written "pages" herself but never sent any, and put most of them in a drawer. She said she'd thought of his ambitions and all he wanted to do. And she had her shame, too, she said.

Shortly before we stood to retire she said she'd thought about it and decided it was only right that our family know about Ned's good friend.

Henry Rutherford had joined a Louisiana regiment, and she'd had a letter from home saying that he was with the Confederates at a battle fought two months before Gettysburg.

She sighed and with a quiver in her voice said, "He was lost, too, dear Henry." She looked out past my shoulder for a few moments. "But it wasn't defending slavery," she said. "Henry no more believed in slavery than Ned."

SIXTEEN

"Octoroon. Occc-toh-roooon. Mulll-la-toh. Qua-droooon." I sat in the garden by the little pool after supper, allowing their lilt, rolling them out in my head. They were like musical terms. But one surely wasn't!

A 'person of color'! How strange. What people ⋯ who were the people without color? And for that matter, what *thing* was there without color?

I raised the backs of my hands, fingers spread. browned from the sun. Which four five months earlier had been white. Or pink. Or at least as much *pink* as white. I broke an inward smile.

Pinkatoon! Martin William Dascomb: Pinkatoon!

But perhaps most of these terms had been brought from music after all. They might have been, for you could look at the notes on a page and tell their value— a quarter, a half. And so too might some have looked at a face and given it a value, identifying someone as ⋯ as what? As one-quarter of ⋯ or no, as *three* quarters of ⋯ a real person. A person *without* color!

How strange!

I thought of Sophie. Was there a "roon" for Sophie? I calculated. A sixteenth! And if she had children ⋯ How many "drops" of blood out of their thousands. Ah but no matter. There was rule for that.

All about was still, other than a bird or two calling across the sea of many-colored blossoms. The air was clear and cool and shining and it felt like being in the midst of some vast jewel. I wondered at such a peace as this. And then I thought of what Isis had said, that it was only people that made no sense.

I watched as a bumblebee wobbled into view ahead, a plump little fellow but a little unsteady on his wings, as if drunk with something. I imagined a bird eyeing him from a nearby branch and rose to advance and quicken him off.

My gaze fell to a patch of tall, spiked flowers below. Pink. But as I held on them they seemed more purple than pink. They were one, then other. Or neither. The words, the names, wouldn't stay put, and the more intently I looked, the more they slipped and slid, almost mockingly. Til it seemed all these thrusting stalks had fixed *me*!

I looked back along the path before wandering outward again. Marie had gone up after dinner to check on Isis—and to see if I might be permitted a very short visit. And if not ... I thought of the slip of paper in my pocket. Ned's poem.

She looked a little somber when I turned at her call. But she told me that Isis was doing well enough for a visit, though I couldn't stay long and wasn't to expect much from her. "But we'll take the rest of your walk first," she said.

She asked if Mama kept a flower garden at home, and I told her she had one by the kitchen and another out behind; I said she kept vases filled in the kitchen and the parlor all the months she could. She stooped to pick up a twig and then wondered aloud what my mother must have thought after reading her letter. It seemed like a beginning of sorts, and I didn't reply at once. She began turning the twig in her hand. "I know there was a girl once, a girl of three, as I recall. Your brother told me about her."

"That was Marcia," I said. "She died before I was born." I waited for more, but when she spoke again it was of Ned. "Your brother thought he might run for office someday, did he tell you that, that he wanted to study the law and set himself up in Concord or Boston?"

I said I'd heard him talking with Mama, but I didn't think he'd have said much around Father. Then I said last Spring, when he'd been home, he went around to some towns making speeches for Lincoln before the election. I said I'd read about one in the Manchester newspaper. "It was on the front page, even," I said.

Oh yes, she smiled. She could see Ned like that, up in front of people. "Even if in some ways I think he was quite shy."

I said Father didn't put up with him much, defending Mr. Lincoln.

The light had begun to mellow, and our shadows led us along the path for a while. Her next thoughts quite surprised me.

"Martin, I do hope it's been a comfort to you, knowing that are not alone in your grief." I fought off a hitch in my step and kept on a pace or two. "God will be sorrowful, too," she said, "at having Ned return to him so soon; I trust you know that."

I fell back slightly.

"God's heart will be broken, too," She said, turning a little.

I quashed an impulse and moved up. But for some reason, then, allowed it: I said it didn't seem like God cared much! Marie took two or three steps ahead before saying she hoped I'd come to feel otherwise someday.

We turned into the sun gleaming alongside one of the big chimneys ahead and went on in our silence past a sundial on a granite pedestal; I saw the gate ahead and thought of the poem in my pocket, but with my earlier words still lingering between us, perhaps, it didn't seem any time for it.

Was it to shake off the weight I'd come to feel and what I sensed in her, too? All at once I stopped and told her I'd brought something, something Ned wrote while he was in the army. I reached into my pocket.

"This is a poem!" I said, holding up the small, folded sheet. "It's about you. Me and Mama both think so!" I held it out.

She looked at me in alarm, then down at my hand, then up again. Then away.

"I'm not ready for this!" she said grimly, staring. "Not now!" I fumbled for something to say. Nothing came.

She whirled to stare at the hand fallen to my side, then turned again and started away, but after a few quick paces she stopped.

"I'm sorry, Martin. I cannot, I cannot right now."

A few minutes later I found her waiting just inside. She apologized. I apologized. She said she'd take whatever I had. She said she'd look at it another time.

"Why don't you go up and see her now," she said.

. . .

I paused at the door, tapped lightly and listened. Tapped again. Then turned the handle cautiously.

She was on her back with a sheet snugged up under her chin. Her eyes were closed. Her face was flushed. Her splayed feet tented the cover. I nudged the door behind to a soft click and whispered. She didn't stir. I took a step in and waited. The room smelled of something medicinal.

"They said I could visit," I breathed.

I looked about. The room was neither large nor small, and barren like my own. And white: walls and ceiling, the few spare furnishings, even the iron bedstead. Everything was white, or at best a pale gray. It felt detached, like being in a cloud. I went to take up a chair and sit in by her.

"You should see this place," I said, for it seemed all along that she was awake. I let her listen. "It's like a castle," I said. "There's big chimneys and a huge carriage house with horses. Such horses, too!" I paused for a sign in her, and with none went on. "And I stayed there one night, above them."

I told her how I'd met Marie and the little girl and how I had played games with her. She gave not the slightest response.

"Ise?" I said.

I sat back. On the wall above the bureau was a small steel engraving of a pond with a clearing above and a woodland border along the top. I squinted to see a deer with its head lowered at a drink. I looked out the window for a time and then whispered to her that maybe I should come another time.

The chair creaked as I rose. But at the door I turned to see that her eyes had opened. She murmured something. A single word.

"What?" I said.

"Don't come," she said to the ceiling.

"Don't come?"

Very slightly her head nodded.

And then, in a flash, I understood. *My hand, my fist.*

I saw them pressed to her there!

"Oh no! I didn't mean it, honest; I didn't know what to do!"

She didn't stir, but I thought I saw tears. I took a step in, then another. I said I wanted to help but I couldn't think how.

"I'm dirty!" she said and struggled to turn away onto her side. "Dirty."

"Dirty? I said. Then my voice rose. "No! It weren't you!"

Too loud! She groaned.

"Don't you understand?" she said with sudden force. "Are you dumb?"

I did understand. I saw an image of the man and glanced away to glare at the headboard's iron bars. "I ain't dumb!" I said. "And it ain't you that's dirty!"

Isis shifted onto her back and gazed up. Then she murmured something and the aching, faraway sound of her pierced me. I sat in toward her and reached out my hand. I held it an inch above her shoulder for a second, then drew it back and leaned in by her ear. "But I hear you, Ise," I said. "I can hear you."

It was all I could say. But it was true, and anything more would not have been true, and I felt that, and I felt everything my poor voice was trying to say beyond the words. And I ached for her to have heard me.

A minute or two later there came a knock at the door, and the servant girl who'd brought tea to the parlor came in, carrying a tray and a fresh towel over her shoulder. She smiled but didn't speak and only went to stand aside and wait.

I stood and told Isis that none of that stuff mattered to me and I was not going nowhere til she got better.

It began to rain an hour or so later. The sky darkened and for a short time there were thunderclaps. In my room on the edge of the bed, it took me an effort to calculate that I had been here now into a third night.

SEVENTEEN

"Sometimes these things are temporary," Marie said, "but this is what we have, and we have to face it."

Isis's fever had risen in the night. I was at a late breakfast on my own and had squeezed my eyes shut at her pronouncement.

"She's a strong girl, Martin" she said. But I knew full well what an uncontrolled fever often led to.

She suggested I let Sophie take me for a walk around the block. Sophie would like that, and she had to go into the city again to confirm a time at the photograph studio, for a look in about my suit, and to send another wire to New Hampshire.

After the first few steps toward the gate, Sophie abruptly changed directions and pulled at my hand. "First yet's make a cake," she said.

She seated herself at the sandbox and looked up at me standing by, preoccupied. "You have to sit *down*!" she said.

A short while later we started up Mountain Street, facing ahead to its end and an open hillside beyond, the beginnings of Mount Royal, from which the city had taken its name. We turned left into a short, quiet street with several three-story, shingled houses on the left behind well kept lawns. Sophie pointed to the first and told me she went there to play sometimes. The wide pale blue sky was streaked with high clouds

Half way along I asked if she'd ever had a shoulder ride. She hadn't, and I told her it was my favorite thing when I was her age. I said my brother used to raise me up high. "Like this," I said, reaching both arms full up. "Then he'd set me down, and off we'd go." I took a quick stride or two away and called over my shoulder. "Just like this!" I stopped and turned.

She stood looking back.

"It's okay," I said. "We don't have to."

She steadied her eyes on me. My own widened. I tilted my head.

"Maybe I can," she said, but doubtfully.

"Or let's just wait til another time," I answered, then watched as her eyes narrowed, frowning.

I began slowly, with her fingers gripping at my temples and her elbows tight to my neck. I kept an easy pace til I felt her relax. She was a slight and slender thing and felt a little like a bird that had privileged me by lighting on a shoulder. When I was certain of her, I added a little spring and began bumping us along. She giggled. Then I thought of myself with Ned and began weaving left and right, back and forth and back, bringing squeals of delight.

She was just like me a lifetime ago!

The empty street ended in another left turn. I stopped to boost her down, and we stood, merry-faced and panting, "This is *just* how I remember it," I beamed down at her, "with my brother when *I* was three!"

"I don't have a brother," she said.

"Yes, I know that."

"Besides, Mammy a'yeady told me you had one."

"She did?"

"Because she knows him."

"*She knows him?*"

"Uh-huh, silly. That's why you *came* here!"

What had Marie told her? Or was there something she'd overheard?

"But what's a sojer?" she said, and repeated it at my silent, fuddled response.

"A soldier?" I said. "Well ⋯ I guess they just wear a special kind of clothes, that's all." I pointed up the road. "Let's go up there," I said and reached for her hand.

"What kyoz?"

"They wear all blue, that's all."

"B'yoo?"

"Dark blue. That's a nice color, isn't it?" Again I reached for her hand, and tugged.

I could sense her still at thought.

"Do you have a job?" she asked.

"Sort of," I said. "I live on a farm, I milk cows."

She halted. "M'yik cows?"

"Sure," I grinned. "Maybe sometime I'll show you, when you get bigger."

"Uncuh George has a job," she said.

"Uncle George? Who's Uncle George?"

"You know! Uncuh *George!*"

"Ah, yes!" I said in sudden recognition of his first name. The master of the house!

This road, too, was vacant, but ahead I could see a wide and busy intersection; no cause yet for concern, but when Sophie let go my hand and skittered off ahead, I called out. She stopped to look back. "Not so far, Sophie," I warned. She turned and set little fists on her hips.

"Oh yook, you!" she cried, pointing out into the yard beyond. "Yook!"

It was a cat crossing the yard, an orange tabby, but my heart had fallen at her term for me. You! Had she forgotten my name?

SHERBROOKE.

My eyes held on the wooden sign at the intersection, and I saw us there again, by the other like this where with a hopeful heart I had told Isis we were almost there.

I told Sophie that she *must* keep hold of my hand here!

"I know-w!" she complained.

We began along a footpath worn into the grass. Not far ahead was a shallow lawn in front of a stone business establishment. But most of the city proper took up on the far side. All along and into the distance was an unbroken wall of brick or granite, three and four-story buildings. Pedestrians bustled up and down on a long, five-foot-wide planked sidewalk. Carriages stood by waiting.

A boy about my age came down from a shop, dressed in high stockings and a simple linen shirt like any one of mine at home. On his head, a baker's cap. He looked about, then tucked a parcel under his arm and launched himself away at a jog. I watched him up the planks—fifty, a hundred yards before he took two or three steps up and disappeared. I felt a pinch of envy at his world, at his purpose.

As we neared the turn back onto Mountain Street, I looked out and was arrested by the sight of a red-stone steeple in the distance, rising gracefully a hundred feet or more til it resolved into a still point. I stood in wonder at its ruddy glow in all the common, surrounding light and felt myself a witness to something vital, almost alive.

But Sophie was saying something.

"I said what are you yooking at?" she said.

I pointed. "That steeple up there. It's beautiful, don't you think so?"

She looked up at me wonderingly and I told her I liked the color. "See how it shimmies a little," I said. She gave me a sigh, and I smiled.

And in silence all along the quarter mile up Mountain Street to the gate she kept a firm hold of my hand.

. . .

At half past two that afternoon we pulled up at 17 Bleury Street, before an imposing granite building set close to the road's edge. I looked out at the long, carved, gold-leaf sign.

THE PHOTOGRAPHIC STUDIOS OF WILLIAM NOTMAN.

Marie and Sophie and I, along with one of the servant girls, had descended into the heart of the city in the three-seated coach that had brought Mr. Drummond back from the railroad depot only an hour before. I had been turned about, smiled at, and pronounced fit: in a new brown tweed suit, starched shirt, and a black cravat the butler had tied under my chin. My gleaming new shoes bound me tightly at both feet.

I remained uncomfortable, and hopelessly self-conscious, but as I watched our driver hand Marie down, I heard Father's voice much as he might have responded to a grumble at the weather.

Well, here you are! What are you gonna do? Where else you gonna go!

The double-wide, heavy oaken door opened directly into a enormous square hall, with a thirty-foot staircase in the center that rose to a three-sided balcony above. Two men had greeted us, and after some small talk, while an attendant led Sophie and Marie off to change into gowns brought in from the coach in a steamer trunk, I was shown to an armchair,.

I had been told to expect a wait and to wander around for a look if I wanted. I sat alone for awhile before going to a row of portraits on a sidewall. I edged along past men, mostly, but several women and a few family groupings; by landscapes, an image of sailing ships at rest, a group of men at a game of curling stones. Several of these had been tinted with color.

Then, toward the rear, I came upon a broad view of the city taken from what surely was the top of Mont Royal; maybe from up behind the

Drummond house, I thought. And here I paused, having seen several spires rising above a sea of rooftops. Would it be here, the one that had earlier transfixed me? I stepped in. And there it was, or so it seemed, beyond the dark branches of a foreground tree. I lingered. But here it looked no different than any of three or four others.

Marie emerged at last - and the sight of her gave me an immediate start. The gown, a satiny golden brown set with darker prints, fit her most snuggly at the waist and all above. Her long arms were bare below the shoulders. Her face was radiant, yet, it struck me, with a trace of sadness showing through.

All this I took in at once, but blushing, I took my head sharply away. Had she read the poem, I thought. Had she read it?

"Now Martin. Surely! Surely you didn't think we'd have you outdo us did you?"

Sophie stood eagerly by, all aglow in a full, light blue gown. Her hair had been done up in yellow bows, one on each side. I rose to her and said how pretty she looked; I said she looked like the sky in that dress. But at once knew I'd missed the mark. "You look like a *princess!*" I said.

"Either one will do," smiled Marie, wryly.

"Martin yooks yike Uncuh George," said Sophie, but the light laughter that followed confused her.

Mr. Fraser, our photographer, was a cheerful, balding man of middle age and common features, although it seemed that someone, his wife perhaps, might have trimmed the tufts of hair in his ears. He led us upstairs to where an assistant stood by a door with a small bronze plaque fixed in the middle.

OPERATING ROOM A.

I stood in the threshold for a few moments, in awe, gazing at an entire wall of high windows. And through them, below and beyond, the city's rooftops and the long sweep of the great river.

But there were more windows, and these set into the very roof itself!. Four or five of them. Long, frosted panels. I gaped, but before Mr. Fraser beckoned us on, saw me still looking up, and took half a minute to explain their purpose.

The room smaller than it had seemed at first, and mostly empty. In the center, behind a four-foot, curved stone bench. stood a large canvas painting of a trellis abundantly hung with vines and leaves and grapes. The camera box on a tripod faced these from six or eight feet away.

Mr. Fraser seated Marie in the center with Sophie and me at her sides. Then Marie said no, she wanted me in the middle, I should be the primary subject here. She turned and told me they already had photographs aplenty of themselves. "Of course. That will do just as well," said Mr. Fraser

A few instructions and cautions about moving followed, then several adjustments to head and body angles. Mr. Fraser shifted back and forth among us til finally he waved a hand at his assistant, who hurried off into a side room, from returned bearing the glass plate in both arms.

"Just so," said Mr. Fraser. "Now, if you please, just hold!" He nodded, and the assistant reached out to remove the lens cap, revealing a three or four inch glass eye.

Sophie sat forward. "But I don't want to!"

"Sophie!" said Marie.

Mr. Fraser's head popped up. "No, no," he said, waving. "It's my fault." He started round. "We should have addressed this."

He went to Sophie, kneeled, and said most kindly, "Would you like me to show you how this works?" Her face held its pout; she didn't answer. "There's nothing to harm," he said quietly. "Come. I'll show you."

It took a minute of persuasive teamwork then, until Mr. Fraser leaned in by the box alongside Sophie to explain how nothing came *out* at all. And there was only this little window that let the light *in*! "That lets us make a picture of you in there," he said.

Sophie stood, still skeptical - and indeed, as it had already struck me, the protruding brass tube certainly looked more like the snubbed barrel of a gun than it did a 'window'.

Mr. Fraser straightened and look down. "I know,' he said. "How would this be? If you can be *really* good, I think we can find something nice for you when we're done."

"What?"

"Oh-h, let's see," he said and with a twinkle glanced at Marie. "I don't suppose you like peppermint, do you?"

"Uh-huh. I do!"

"Well then ... are you ready?"

I could almost see Sophie holding his eyes. Then she said in her little voice, "Can Martin have some, too?"

• • •

He sat thirty feet away in an armchair before a wide hearth. Only the back of his head was visible, and I caught the scent of cigar smoke just as a plume of it rose from him.

Marie had taken me directly to the library when we returned from the studio. But this clearly wasn't the time, I thought, and gave her a distressful glance. My feet felt hot and cramped. "We'll only a be minute," she said and called to announce us.

Books! Scores of them! Hundreds! On high shelves running the whole length of the sidewall on the right.

With books I felt most truly at home, and so here at once I felt almost as much as I needed to about this man. I thought of Sunbeam, my old friend.

Mr. Drummond was a man of early middle age, and about my height, not much above five and a half feet. He had thickly-lashed, rust-colored brow, and a matching mustache that drooped well past his mouth on both sides, features that added considerably to his height and made him a most imposing sight.

It was a brief, cordial introduction and ended with an invitation to dine with him and with Mrs. Drummond a few hours later. And only then, at the mention of the lady, did the appreciable difference in their ages strike me.

Upstairs I loosened my tie and pulled of my shoes; I sat on the edge of the bed.

And then it flooded back. *Isis might die!*

• • •

Three tall vases of flowers divided the twelve-foot dining table. Gas-lit wall sconces cast faint shadows into the snowy linen. The high windows beyond looked out into the evening light. We took seats in carved walnut chairs with Mr. Drummond at the head, the two ladies on his left, and me on the right. Onion soup with a browned, cheese topping came first, and after some minutes of small talk, Mr. Drummond brought up my acquaintance with Shadrach Minkins.

"Here's something you wouldn't know of him," he said. "He may be the most expensive barber in all of Montreal! And why? I asked him once and he told me it wasn't so much for the monetary gain - you can see the modest shop he keeps - but rather for what it did for him professionally. He said it kept him sharp, kept him focused on his patrons and what they wanted. He said he tried to remember the little things about them. It made a difference, he thought."

He had been looking at me intently, though not unkindly, as it felt, and it wasn't difficult to hold his gaze.

"Now that is an impressive fellow," he went on. "And he's right, you know. Most of us think it's big things that make for success. But it isn't; it's in the details."

"I think Mr. Drummond wishes he'd been a teacher," said the Lady, smiling - to which, indulgently, he returned a smile of his own.

"Anyway. You've met our Shadrach, and I hear it's a most fortunate thing you did."

I thought of Isis as she stood uphill from me in Manchester. *I don't guess it's any luck at all.*

The bowls were cleared and a silver platter of roast lamb and jelly brought along with others of oval-shaped potatoes, and minted peas. Mr. Drummond brought up Ned, briefly, and then Isis, and like the Lady, it was by way of acknowledgment and he expected nothing of me.

The lady asked him to tell us about what he'd seen in Toronto. The city was about half the size of Montreal, he said, though growing rapidly. And he said he'd visited a new cathedral that was nearly finished, that lacked only the top of its spire and the installation of bells, which again put me in mind of my encounter a few hours earlier.

They had questions about home and the farm. And then school. And I said I'd always liked it, at least until the teacher I'd had for years had gone off and we'd gotten another. Mr. Drummond didn't take that up and asked instead about my subjects, then books and stories I liked. His brows lifted when I said I'd been reading *Oliver Twist*.

"Ah, yes, Mister Dickens!" he said sitting back. "I've met the man, you know. And a very clever fellow he is ⋯ in conversation as well as his writing; quite capable of promoting himself," he said with a wry smile."

For the next five minutes we talked about *Oliver Twist*, and his enthusiasm again put me in mind of Mr. Partridge —so much so that the mustache I'd found intimidating, began to look out of place in a man capable of his almost boyish indulgence.

Mrs. Drummond said that she'd told her husband how I'd had a chance to spent time with Sophie. It seemed an invitation, so I mentioned the games, and our walk. I thought better of saying that she reminded me a little of my brother.

"She calls me Uncle George, you know," said Mr. Drummond, with a gleam in his eye. "But I think that honor belongs to you, doesn't it?"

All at once, as somehow it hadn't before, it struck me that the Drummonds had no children of their own! And then I knew, of course, how it was that Sophie appeared to consider herself quite the little center here.

Dessert was Mr. Drummond's favorite, I was told: a fruity, Scottish cake called Dunesslin Pudding. And then, having finished it, Mr. Drummond surprised me by asking if I would sit with him in the library. I glanced across at Marie, who returned a smile.

"I won't keep you long. But I would like to know a little more about you, if I may." His tone was earnest, but I felt the trace of affection in it.

We left the ladies to the last of their wine, and in the library as we passed along the dark wall of books, I wondered if there might be as many here as in the whole of the Peterborough Town Library! Mr. Drummond gestured at one of the leather armchairs and went to a sideboard to take a decanter and fill a short-stemmed crystal glass. He turned and said, looking down at me, "Let me say right off that it was a foolish thing you did in coming here. I suppose you know that." My eyes went wide. "Any rational man would say so, and he'd be right," he said and started forward, then halted, smiling. "At the same time, you know, he might be wrong!"

He sat himself on the front edge of the chair and faced me at an angle. I held my gaze in the space between him and the hearth.

"There's an old saying, though I don't suppose you've heard of it. Never foolish, never wise," he said.

"No, sir."

"No. And it'll be a while before you think of yourself as wise. Only to be expected," He raised the glass and passed it back and forth under his nose before taking a first small taste. "Not wise yet," he went on, "but from what I hear it took some courage to come all this way." He settled back into the chair and crossed his legs. "We'll leave it at that," he said. "Not *merely* foolish, not *only* that." He took another sip, then said with a slight smile, "You know, that old saying may be true, but I'd wager it's most often used by old men to justify some youthful misadventure."

In the short silence, he rubbed at his chin, and I felt him turn more intent.

"I do have a purpose, and I'll be blunt if I may. I want to know what you've found here. What you've found ⋯ is it what you expected?"

Found? What I'd found?

He gathered himself, apologized, and said he'd start over. "Perhaps you'd tell me what you like to do or what you're good at, that sort of thing."

I shrugged, but he held a patient smile til I told him it was mostly playing ball - and reading, I guessed. Then, I glanced over my shoulder and said I'd never seen so many books as this. He waited, til I said my brother liked books, too. I turned and to look into the hearth and say I thought it came from my mother.

"Books," he said. "And education. You could do worse than that." He uncrossed his legs and sat forward. "It brings something to mind, and if you will, perhaps I might tell you a little story ⋯ about my own education."

He said he'd been about my age and away from home at a well regarded school for boys, and one day he and a few chums had a small fire get away from them and burn a shed to the ground.

"We had a choice," he said. "The headmaster told us we could commit ourselves to rebuilding that little barn or be expelled." He paused to take the last of his brandy. "We wrote letters home explaining what we had done and had to do to make it right. And the short of it is that I found myself in charge of the whole matter: Obtaining funds, bringing the boys and a few men together, arranging the times to work. All of it" He looked down at the glass in his hand, then set it on the arm of his chair. "It was one of those youthful adventures I spoke of," he said.

My eyes followed after him when he stood and went to the cabinet. He had an aim. I knew he did and tightened, wondering at it.

Without refilling his glass, he turned. "It started that way, as a misadventure," he said, "but I learned more from that than anything in my books or classrooms. I learned that I was good at organizing people, and it became my life's work." He returned to his chair and leaned in toward me with hands clasped loosely between his knees. He tipped his head. "Now from this journey of yours, I don't suppose you'll discover your life's work, but *something* will come of it." He looked at me intently.

"I don't know, sir, Maybe, I hope."

"And you *came* for something," he said. "Was it what you expected, what you've found here?"

I stared at my hands. I saw Mama's face. Her face and the awful distance in it. And her hand with Marie's letter in it slipped to her side.

"I wanted to see them," I murmured.

"See them."

"I made a box for my mother," I said.

"You made a box, for your mother."

"She hasn't seen it, it isn't finished yet. I just wanted to make her something."

"Make something," he said, shifting to face me more directly. "You wanted to make something."

"I wanted to help my friend, too," I said. Then my voice broke as I said she didn't have much.

He stood after a minute or so, after letting me settle.

"Let me tell you what I think," he said. "I think you are that girl's best bet. I think we ought to keep you here another day or two if we can."

In the entry a short while later he told me that McGill College was just around the block and that it wouldn't be hard to arrange a tour, if I wanted.

. . .

I awoke to the strokes of a bell from beyond the open window—from the clock tower at McGill College, I learned later. It wasn't past midnight, I hadn't slept long. I lay on my back, alert, gazing up into the stillness. I thought of Mr. Drummond, remembered dreaming of him shallowly, thought of his solicitous turn with me and what he'd said about Isis. I thought of horses and how if only she could ⋯

Then something possessed me. I thrust myself up and sat for a second, reached for my trousers, pulled them on, and my shirt. I went barefoot to the door and stopped to take a hard breath.

I looked down the hall to see an edge of light under the door. I went ahead on forefeet. I stopped. The door seemed like a sheet of iron. What was I doing! My head fell to my chin. I turned in and sank against the wall.

I don't know how long it was til the door opened, but the shock passed between the two of us like a current.

Marie glared down into my upturned face, then turned to pull the door shut.

"This will not do!" she said. She looked away and sighed heavily, then again, then motioned me to follow her down the hall. She had a lamp and was dressed in a bedcap and long robe. At the top of the staircase she pointed me to sit.

"You simply *cannot* do this! It is near midnight!"

I told her I couldn't sleep and watched as her expression softened.

"Well," she said, "she's no worse, I can tell you that. Maybe this thing has reached its limit."

She hoped that might help me feel better, at least enough to get back to sleep. She asked if a glass of milk would help.

I didn't answer. I told her Isis had said she was dirty.

Marie looked at me, then down into the emptiness below, and it was most a minute before she replied. It was what women did in these circumstances, she said. She said Isis had taken everything, all of it, on herself.

"But it ain't *her* that's dirty!"

"Did you tell her that?"

I said I had. I said I'd all but shouted it.

"Well, that make two of us, she said, and smiled. "But I didn't shout." Once more she asked about milk. I shook my head and thanked her. She looked off below again and after a while she spoke again into the darkness below, "I don't suppose you've ever wondered what kept me from writing to him."

I drew up but didn't answer; it had felt only in part a question.

"It takes a long time," she said. "A long time to feel whole again. And even now ... " She looked up. "Even now. All the pain, all the trouble I've brought your family when you hardly ..."

"Oh no!" I blurted. "I think it *saved* Mama!"

EIGHTEEN

I didn't come down in the morning til after nine! After Marie had left Sophie at a friend's house and gone in to the city; after the doctor had looked in on Isis; and after Mr. Drummond, before leaving for his office, had asked the butler to go over to McGill College and arrange a tour. A young man came by for me at eleven.

McGill was smaller than I remembered Dartmouth College, where once with Mama I had visited Ned some years before. It was a welcome diversion, and I felt the tug of academic gravity from the cluster of five or six brick and stone buildings, and from the eager faces of young men passing by with heavy books in hand.

Early that afternoon Marie led Sophie and me into the dining room. She uncoiled the tie from a large manila envelope and drew out three ten-inch square cards. Cabinet Portraits, she termed them.

"There we are!" exclaimed Sophie," as her mother nudged at them til they were just so, an inch or two apart on the table.

"And don't we look grand!"

I'd already decided I looked like someone at a funeral.

I sit at my desk now some twelve years on, having spent a minute with the framed image on the wall to my left. And forever, there, will I sit up woodenly straight with my hands in my lap, fingers interlaced, and with all weight in my heart discernable only to me in the flat mask of my face. In Sophie's doll-like face I see a lingering trace of her mistrust; in Marie's, a placid calm, and perhaps the hint of a smile.

"Yes, these'll do just fine," Marie said, and then to me "Two of these will be yours to take home."

Two? I thought for an instant. But then, with a sudden glow within, there was no need to ask why.

"Has your family had anything taken?" Marie asked.

I thought of the CDV Ned had sent home from Virginia, the one in its cowhide frame on Mama's bureau, with him seated partly to one side in his lieutenant's coat, with his long hands and fingers together at his lap and his hair slicked down and parted neater than usual. It didn't seem the time to speak of it, and I told her no, the family had never sat all together like this.

A maid came into the entry and beckoned for Marie, who returned, bright-faced, a minute later.

"Her fever's broken. It's gone!" she said.

"Don't go in all a'bluster, you hear!" Marie had insisted. And before the back staircase I paused, much as I'd been taught to do in the milkroom at home.

I knocked.

The voice was thin and hoarse. "Come in, Marty."

The room itself had changed. A vase of red and yellow gladiolus—gladioli?—stood on the bureau. Another, of pink roses sat on the side table by Isis' head; the air smelled fresh and floral. An amber curtain held a warm glow.

Her face was still swollen, but the flush had given way to a kind of waxy gray. She wore no bonnet now, and her hair, what was left of it, stood out as if recently washed.

She turned to me, winced, and then smiled.

"I have a headache," she said. "But hello, Marty."

"Hello to *you*!" I said.

Her fingers, soft and plump, still looked like someone else's.

"You look better," I said.

"Some, I ain't gonna die anyhow."

And that was the last of my containing myself.

"Ace! OH, ACE!" I cried.

I went to the small chair and pulled it up by her. I told her I had lots to tell when she wanted. I said she didn't have to talk but just listen. I sat down quietly and waited.

"That lady, she's been up here," she said.

"Marie? You mean Marie."

She gave a shallow nod, but didn't say more.

"She's done by me, too," I said. "And all these people. They have; I could tell you some things all right."

"Okay."

I didn't where to begin. I said I'd just seen a photograph we'd had taken. "It was Marie and me and Sophie, the little girl, and they dressed me up in this new suit, you would have doubled over. I was like the Prince of Wales or something and Marie was on the one side, and Sophie, and we had to sit, but then Sophie . . ." I halted.

"Take a breath," she said.

I told her about the events of the last days, and at the end I told her I'd given the poem to Marie.

"I know," she said.

I sat up. "What? You know?"

"She didn't dare read it."

"She *told* you that?"

"She told me a lot. And about Ned."

I almost asked what.

"She was going to read it now maybe."

"Now? Was it *you*?"

She didn't answer.

I sat back and looked at her in wonder. She asked if I would pour her some water, then worked herself up some to take the tumbler in both hands.

"Your mother's gonna be happy," she said after she'd finished and held out the glass. "You got something to bring her."

Before I left I told her it had felt like two worlds here, one downstairs, where I had been treated beyond anything, but up here by her room, and in mine, it was like a nightmare.

I went down the hall into my room. Closed the latch behind and stood, then let go in sobs.

• • •

Marie took Sophie and me for a sunset walk up the road toward Mount Royal. Where the road bent left, Sophie left the doll's carriage she'd pushed along and we started up a grassy lane. The low clouds ahead were streaked with pink and orange.

When Sophie skittered off ahead, I thought it a good time to ask what would now become of Isis. Marie didn't know but said there was no need to rush.

"I will tell you this, she won't go back; not before I've heard more from your mother. We'll have to work on ⋯ I don't know what!"

But *you*!" she said into my somber silence. "I think we both know it's time for you. I'm thinking of the day after tomorrow, and I've begun with a letter to take with you."

"Yook!" Sophie called, holding up a fistful of black-eyed Susans. Marie returned a wave.

She said she hoped she hadn't neglected me terribly much and I said, oh no, she hadn't. I said I knew what she'd done for Isis.

"She heard a lot. And I don't know that she spoke two words. But ⋯ I think she gave me as much as anything I did by her."

We had slowed and she had been gazing up the hill beyond Sophie. Now she stopped and turned to me.

"I wonder if we might think of what's happened here as … " She looked off.

"What?" I said. She took a few moments, then said she'd tell me and hoped I might forgive her if it didn't seem the right kind of thing to say.

"I was going to say a gift," she said. "Your coming here with her. And you. Like a last gift from him."

"A little like he was here," I said. I told her I'd felt like that sometimes. Then I told her what Jim Henry had said about remembering Ned.

"Except, you had to see Jim's face," I said. "Even more than the words."

She drew a long breath and brushed at her forehead. She said Sophie had taken a good nap earlier, but it was well past her bedtime. Then she called.

On the way back Sophie stopped to pick a few stems of Queen Anne's Lace. "These are for your friend," she said, "cuz she's not sick anymore."

We turned through the gate and Marie asked if I'd like to have a glass of that ginger ale.

NINETEEN

I spent one more day at the big stone house in Montreal. I had better luck at Hide and Seek with Sophie and took dinner again with Marie and the Drummonds, where I heard the Lady called Zella! I would have imagined her as Margaret or Elizabeth or Harriet. Zella would have better fit Sophie. And Mr. Drummond told me that if I had a mind to it, he'd be pleased to see me at McGill College someday.

Afterward I sat with Isis for a second time that day. It wasn't long. We'd already talked about how we'd been through some things, and I don't think either of us dared bring up the future. I assured her I'd to speak to my mother and father and thank them. But what pained me then, and even now, was my failure of courage. Her hand lay at rest on the summer coverlet and came to occupy half my attention. I had wanted to reach and hold it, and did not.

I lay on the bed that night and pictured Father meeting me in Manchester. And I saw Mama coming out onto the porch at home when we arrived. But at some point my mind took a leap back, and I saw the twins that day at school, hollering up about the fighting in Pennsylvania. I marveled at how long ago it seemed and how much had happened in - I worked at the arithmetic. Six, six weeks. Scarcely more than a tenth of one year.

I returned to Father and thought how I'd manage myself with him. Oddly, I didn't feel anxious. Something in me felt changed. And perhaps even then I'd begun the long process of understanding my father a little differently.

• • •

I woke to the chitter of birds and the early purple light in the window. I felt fresh, and wondered at when I'd last felt that way. I dressed in the new jacket and trousers Marie had insisted I wear (she excused me the cravat).

I sat on the edge of the bed to wait. Before me the stood the strapped, leather case Mr. Drummond had brought down the night before. "Bring it back when you return," he'd said to dismiss the last of my protests. I rose at the sound of Marie's footsteps in the hallway. I held my eye on Isis' door, as we approached. I didn't suppose she'd be awake but raised a hand as we passed by.

The house was still but for the movements of a maid or two by the kitchen. I ate a hasty breakfast, though not without taking a second helping of stewed pears, then even a last large spoonful. At six a.m. I climbed into the carriage to sit in the rear with Marie, and as we turned left out of the gate, I looked over my shoulder for a last glance at the lordly house.

My stomach tightened as my thoughts turned to the one last 'good-bye' ahead. Partings had always been awkward for me; I had often stood by marveling at the ease of some, or most, with them.

We spent most of the short trip in silence, and it seemed that Marie was as much absorbed in her own thoughts as I was at mine. She hadn't mentioned the poem as yet, but I felt certain she would.

We stopped at the ticket window, then crossed diagonally through the hall toward an arched portal with an eight-inch brass numeral above. The station was surprisingly busy with passengers and working men pushing or pulling carts loaded with parcels, or with crates full vegetables and fruits. One fellow halted before another and let go a good-humored volley of something in French. I looked at Marie, and she said he'd told his friend that he'd better think about a rocking chair if that was all he could manage.

At the car, by the iron steps, we turned to one another. She said she supposed I didn't need any reminding about crossing the bridge. Then her expression firmed.

"I've read the poem," she said. "And I'm glad I didn't wait because I want you to know what I think. I won't expect you to understand this, but to me they are as much about Sophie as they are about me."

My eyes spread in wonder. Hers glistened.

"He didn't know, of course. But that's how I choose to see it."

I wanted to tell her, as our eyes held, that I understood. But I didn't, not til I thought hard on it on the train.

She took me at the shoulders then and smiled broadly. "All right now, get on with you," she said. "We haven't seen the last of each other." She pulled me to her, quickly and hard, but not long.

I returned her wave as the train jerked and began to pull away. I settled back and waited til we were across the river and out of the tunnel before bringing the case down from the rack to change from my new shoes to the buckled brogans I'd bought in Manchester.

• • •

The day had turned cloudy, and by the time I arrived in Manchester sometime after seven o'clock, the evening had already begun to deepen. Father was out on the platform. I saw him standing familiarly, with his head tipped back slightly and his chin jutting. But his shoulders were drawn inward and down, making him seem smaller. And as we drew closer and banged to a stop, I looked out at a solemn and careworn face.

Is this what I'd brought on!

I stepped down, caught his eye, and halted to throw up an eager hand. I waved. His expression didn't change, but he raised an arm at me.

He looked me up and down

"Well ain't you a sight!" he said with a sly grin. "All dressed up like a spare bedroom."

He reached out and whisked at one my shoulders. The grin broadened.

"The soot on them trains," he said. "Seems a practical man wouldn't go off spruced up as all that."

For the next three hours Father said little while Chub labored us toward and then around Butternut Mountain to the road home. I waited for the stern words; none came, nor any declaration of a punishment. I answered questions about the train ride, the country up north, the kind of farms I saw, but nothing about Montreal or what I'd found or done. It wasn't the beginning I expected.

But Mama's greeting was entirely predictable: a clasp of bear-like strength, a radiant face; joy and relief; a few minutes of this before she beckoned me inside while Father went to the barn with Chub.

She seated me to a supper of cod chowder and green beans. I started to tell her about the suit, and she allowed me a minute before saying all that could wait. Father joined us and told me nothing much had happened, except one of the heifers had caught ill and he hoped she wouldn't have to be put down.

I gave them Marie's letter before I went upstairs for the night.

. . .

Two or three days went by. I had told most everything, from the Irish boys, to Shadrach Minkins, to the gate before the house, to Marie and Sophie and the Drummonds. Father, had heard it all, with some comment but little judgment. I waited for his chastisement and a scripture-introduced consequence for my misadventure. But these, too, never came. One thing only was given me beyond my usual duties: Father had me wash the long row of grimy windows in the cow barn, insisting that I scrub and wipe them clean to shining, inside and out. It was a task never performed by anyone in my memory, and I puzzled at the intent, Once or twice in those small, indirect ways of his he showed approval my work. And once or twice, too, he sounded almost grandfatherly when he spoke to me.

I have a great regret that I never spoke to Father about the difference I saw in him. I had loved my father but feared him nearly as much, and it may have been lingerings of that that kept me from approaching. But Father had never been one for introspection, and I think he would have turned away an inquiry or a kindly assertion if I'd been capable of it. Perhaps I spared him the distress as much as I did myself.

But there was something else I didn't know then.

It would be four months after that summer of '63 when Mama and I learned that Father was most likely already in an early stage of the illness that would rapidly consume him after the first of the year. He never let anything on, of course, until it couldn't be avoided. And in the years since then I have come to believe that life, Father's life, even while it had begun to leave him, may have given him something in return.

. . .

The first week or two of September brought none of the usual relief from the summer's heat. Mama smiled at one of my complaints and said that, well, at least the hummingbirds were staying longer at her garden.

The October reds and yellows lit the hills and the twin maples between the house and barn. A round of harvest suppers and church socials began, and at one of these I gave a recitation of a poem by Mr. Alexander Pope, after which Mama took me about among the women to enjoy their marvel at how I'd remembered all those lines (with no mention of the several times I'd paused to consult the script in my hand).

And *my* but hadn't I grown!

In October another letter arrived from Marie.

Dear Martin,

Isis is showing herself quite able with the horses, just as you said she would. Henri says she's a natural and the quickest learner he's seen. Even I can see how the mares respond to her.

Sophie has taken to her, too, though I don't think Isis enjoys the sandbox as much as you. The other day the two of them came in wearing wreaths of purple and white flowers most cleverly woven together. They came parading through the kitchen like a pair of queens, at least Sophie did.

I've encouraged Isis to write a few lines to include with my own, but she has seemed reluctant. Perhaps she'd respond if you wrote to ask how she fares.

Someone I know had a letter from our friend Robert, He went to Boston, as I think you know. He joined a colored regiment, and I feared it might have been the one caught up in that awful slaughter by the sea in South Carolina. It turns out he did join that outfit, but didn't get there in time for the battle. It seems he is faring well so far, but I am hoping you might join me in praying for him.

Now let me respond to your question. You asked what made me think that God might have need of us at times. I would answer with some evidence for it. For did God not need a woman to bear His son and to be his mother? And did He not need Jesus as a grown man to show us who our Lord truly is and what He wants for us? I believe so and that in our lives we may be able to offer some small comfort to our Maker. Are we not a little like actors in a play and Him the audience? So yes, I do believe that God asks you and me to do His good work, just as He did your brother.

Sophie has come in by my elbow just now, and she instructs me, as you might well imagine, to tell you that Uncle George has given her shoulder rides, but that he doesn't bounce like you!

Please remember me fondly to your mother and father. I know you will. With love, Marie

I knew why Isis was reluctant to write, of course: She was terrible with words! At least of the written sort. Her spelling had always amazed me, and I remember her saying once that it was hard to get what she was thinking "to the end of the pencil." Still, I thought I should send her a few lines. I had thought of her mother several times, and about the possibility of getting some communication to her, though it seemed improbable.

From my exchanges with Marie, and as week followed week, I began to allow myself some optimism about Isis. Mama, too, had had some correspondence with Marie, and from that came the greatest hope, even if she would only tell me that any plans for Isis were not yet firm.

. . .

Then one day, late in the month when the leaves were all down and the birds had gone south, there came an invitation on a card from the Governor's office in Concord.

The State of New Hampshire requests the honor of including the family of Lieutenant Edmund Dascomb in its delegation to attend the dedication of the National Cemetery in Gettysburg, Penn.

Along with this, signed by the Governor himself, was a short note with dates and a statement that the rail fare and lodging expenses would be provided by the state.

Father said that Mama and I should surely go, but it wouldn't be possible for him to take four days away from the farm.

TWENTY

I handed Mama down from the cars at Gettysburg at midafternoon on the eighteenth of November, six days after my fourteenth birthday. She was dressed in her mourning black, but with a new cape and velvet bonnet. I felt smart enough, indeed, in my Montreal suit, and in the shoes I'd worn to passable comfort after half hour stints in them about the house. Mama had spent the journey in surprisingly good spirits, no doubt the result of new friendships and the conversational solace of the women who had also lost sons in the battle.

The thirty of us in the New Hampshire contingent made scarcely a dent in the swarms of people both within the station and outside on the streets. All was abuzz in anticipation the arrival of none other than Mr. Lincoln himself, whose train was already an hour or two late.

It was only a few hundred yards to the Excelsior Hotel, where Mama and I settled ourselves into a small third-floor room. A half hour later we found directions and went out again to walk south toward the new cemetery. It didn't take long; within minutes we were out of the village and standing below a deep slope filled with row upon row of precisely spaced white tablets. Hundreds of them, maybe a thousand!

"And these are all ours!" Mama marveled. "Goodness knows where they put those other fellows."

Under a lightly overcast sky I looked outward to the west into a vast, open expanse of tawny autumn yellow. Perhaps a half mile away to the west stood a long line of leafless trees, and well beyond, a range of low, bluish mountains.

Out here, somewhere out here in all this emptiness was where Ned and our men of the Second had fought. I scanned about for an orchard, for a "knob" of land, as I'd heard it described. I slowed my eye, squinted, went out and back and around. Then I looked deeper still and found a low hump alone in the distance.

Was it there, just there?

"Oh, up there," Mama said, pointing uphill to the cemetery's crest where eight or ten men worked at hammering together a twenty-foot square platform. "I expect that's where we'll get a look at Mr. Lincoln tomorrow. And there'll be a whole lot of folks out here; more'n I've ever been around."

There were other pairs like us, several of them scattered about the hillside, walking the rows, one or two standing side by side with bowed heads. "Shall we go up?" Mama said.

We'd been told the approximate location of the New Hampshire section, and it wasn't long til we looked down a row of stones bearing the shallow-cut names of the '5TH NH VOL'.

Suddenly I didn't want this! My teeth clenched. I turned sharply and took four or five fierce strides away.

"Martin!"

I halted. And stared.

"Martin?" she called.

"NO!"

"We don't have to now," she said solicitously. "We'll go back if you like." She sounded like syrup.

"No!"

"Let's do," she said. "Come. Please!"

"I'm not a baby, Mama!" I said, whirling to glare at her.

"No. you're not," she said quietly. "You're a young man now."

"Ain't that neither!" I said to my feet.

"Oh, I don't know. I bet your brother would think so, I think he would."

I looked down into the village, detesting it and all this whole place.

Mama let me stand - til I took and held the longest breath of my life.

I looked back at her soft, patient face. Then it crept into me and it felt as if Ned himself was looking back at me. I told her I was okay; I told her I was ready.

And once I'd stepped down and began along, it took fewer than ten stones til I found it.

> **Lieut. E. Dascomb**
> **Co. G, 2nd NH Vol.**

After a minute her hand slipped from my shoulder, and sounding almost reverent she told me that she'd brought something. She went into her handbag.

"This is a fish hook," she said, holding up a tiny rusted pin. "What's left of it, at least."

There was no barb and only a little of the curve remained. She held it out in her palm. "I've been thinking of leaving this here, "she said. "I hadn't made up my mind, but I thought I'd tell you the story of it, and then we can decide together."

Ned was eight or nine years old, and one day he'd come running up from the river with this hook gone into the side of his thumb. "All the way past the barb!" Mama said with a grimace. "But he'd kept himself brave til he saw the look of me." She smiled wistfully. "Just a mother's face, don't you know. But it gave him room to go to all pieces.

Well didn't he go hopping all about in the kitchen until we got your father; and then there weren't nothing to do but push the thing futher along til the barb come through so's he could snip it."

We winced at each other, with Mama still smiling, even if I could not. She said she didn't know what became of the barb, but Ned had kept this half in his desk upstairs. And then, years later when she'd all but forgotten it, it had fallen from a Saint Valentine's Day card Ned mailed to her during his first year at the college. And on the card he'd written, *Mama, I'm hooked! Won't you be my Valentine?*

Mama's face was warm now as she told me she'd kept it herself and later sent it back in a letter of her own.

"And I said, 'I'm thinking of you and everything you've put me through.'"

"You said that, Mama!"

She tipped her head back and looked down her nose at me. "Why not?" she said. She said the pin had been back and forth between them three or four times over the years. "It was just a little thing between us," she said and reached into the envelope for a sheet of notepaper. "He left this on my pillow when he was home last, on the day he went back to the army." She handed it to me.

Mama, I'm all out of pointed comments. Thanks for the understanding of your oldest little boy.

"Your oldest little boy," I said. I had the sense of it, but I wanted to hear from her.

"Oh yes. It just means there's still a part of the boy left, even when he grows older; every mother knows that." She paused. "*Some* men do," she said with a mischievous eye. "They come to know that if they're wise."

For an instant I thought of Mr. Drummond and what he'd told me.

Mama looked beyond. "What'll we do with this? Leave it here, shall we?"

"No!" I said at once.

"Oh my," she said a little teasingly. "Take it back? Don't you s'pose it's his after all?"

"We can both keep it, " I said. "Half way. In his room. In his desk."

"Well now, that's an idea, isn't it. That's an idea."

She looked away and was still.

I watched her raise a finger to the corner of an eye.

"Let me set this with him for a minute," she said turning back. "By myself, if I may."

A short while later we made our way down the slope, and at the bottom by the gate Mama stopped.

"I think Ned would approve of something," she said. "For a while now I've thought about moving his desk into your room." I straightened. "Oh just for the use of it, you know! I think Ned would want that, don't you?"

. . .

The following afternoon I stood myself as high as I could on a three-railed wooden fence and looked up over the backs of a thousand heads at the white-haired man at the front of a dais stuffed shoulder-to-shoulder with dignitaries—one of whom, two rows behind, was a most weary-looking President Lincoln.

Edward Everett bowed, and bowed again, smiling appreciatively into all the shouting and clapping below. His head was all agleam, as if the sun itself gloried in his effort. He had spoken for two hours or more, and exhaustingly, for his bold, sometimes booming voice had plainly weakened toward the end. And it seemed, too, that he had exhausted his audience, whose own charged emotions had to have been mixed with relief—as were my own—as he took his bows. His subject, the great battle that had been fought here, he had covered from A to Z in alternately soaring and lilting detail as he gave tribute to both individual and collective heroism.

And now, now? What was there anyone might say or add after such a performance as this! I'm sure I wasn't alone in asking it. Poor Mr. Lincoln would try.

But first a glee club assembled to render something impressively somber. Then a short, thick man with a menacing look thrust himself out front and bellowed.

"The President of the United States!"

And now here he was, the stooped and haggard-looking President, working his way forward, and just at the front in his rumpled long-tailed coat, turning sideways to squeeze himself through.

I should say that I'd had a brief glimpse of him the night before and had been sorely troubled to see so ordinary a fellow. Worse! A man so pale, so sunken of face as to seem close to his end.

He wore a broad, if sorrowful smile. I squinted to see that his spectacles looked as though they might slide off his nose. He nudged them back and waited for the applause and a few calls from below to subside. He stood himself tall and raised a page up under his chin, then lowered it.

A rasping, high-pitched voice, though not especially loud, cut straight through to me at the far reaches.

And then he was saying some things, some things that sounded nice enough, even if I found them a little puzzling. But I had barely gotten past the shrillness in his voice when he stopped, looked up, bowed sheepishly, then raised a hand and began backing away.

He was done, finished!. And almost nothing had registered in me. Nor in anyone, it seemed. The whole throng appeared stunned, and for several long moments a deep silence hung in the air. Heads turned to others in the crowd. Someone hollered uphill, "IS THAT ALL?"

A general murmur arose, and then, at the front, came the beginnings of applause. It spread and swelled and then rose into volleys of cheer and hard-smacked hands.

• • •

Mama and I left Gettysburg early the next morning, and much later, as we approached New York City, I picked up a copy of the *Philadelphia Inquirer* from an empty seat. The president's address was printed on the front page. I leaned in to the side of the bench to steady my hand, then gave up and went back to sit with Mama.

Four score and seven years ago our Fathers established upon this continent a government subscribed in liberty and dedicated to the fundamental principle that all mankind are created equal by a good God . . .

It might have been what I'd heard but still sounded inflated. Stuffy, I thought.

. . . The world will little know and nothing remember of what we see here, but we cannot forget what these brave men did here. It is for us the living to be here dedicated. We owe this offering to our dead. We imbibe increased devotion to that cause for which they gave the last measure of devotion; we here might resolve that they shall not have died in vain.

I nudged at Mama. "Do you know what 'imbibe' means?"
She'd been gazing out the window, absorbed. She turned slowly.
"Imbibe," I repeated. "Do you know that word?"
"Yes-s," she answered wearily. "I guess it means to drink something."
"Uh ... I don't think so, Mama." I read the last several lines to her, emphasizing the phrase about imbibing devotion. "That doesn't seem to be about drinking," I said.
"No," she said and sighed. "It doesn't. But it sounds about right."
A minute passed, and I had set the paper aside when Mama sat herself erect and turned to me with hard eyes.
"I'll tell you what that man was talking about," she said. He was talking about our Ned, that's exactly what he was doing up there." She turned away.
"And he was talking about you!" she said.

A BRIEF AFTERWARD

The day after Christmas we moved Father downstairs to the parlor where it was easier to attend to him, and where it seemed most natural to read to him from the old family Bible we set by him on the stand. He remained true to his nature, taciturn, uncomplaining, stoic. And at times humorous. Once, when we replaced the vase of flowers by him, he made reference to the air in the room by playfully asking why we hadn't ever thought about bringing flowers into the barn when clearing the gutters behind the cows. His last two or three days were reduced to only the rise and fall of his chest. He died at the beginning of February in the New Year.

One thing about that time still puzzles me. Toward the end, when his face had sunk to cheekbone and transparent skin, I came in once, and then again to find my father wearing a beatific smile, and I ventured to say that he looked pleased at something. His eyes opened weakly and he made an effort at raising a hand, as if readying to speak.

But he didn't, or couldn't, and since then I have wondered: As the end approached, had Father come to some new awareness? Or had he only become more certain of something he already knew? I have gone from one sense - or wish for it - to the other.

We buried Father up on the hill by Marcia. The day was a mild one for February, and during our slow upward trek and then throughout the modest service, a soft snow fell in wafers, sifting through the late morning gray to settle and melt into the darker stones.

I have a last, short tale to relate about my father. It is one of my strongest early memories of him, and I include here in light of the difference I saw in him after my return from Montreal. Its ironic resonance may only be a creation of my own, but I choose to honor it anyway, for myself, if not for my father.

One day, when I was perhaps four years old, I came out of the house and looked up to see an immense, blue-black bank of clouds coming on in the western sky. In the midst of it I saw the tossing, giant head of a horse with a dark hole of an eye and a gaping mouth. I stood for a moment in awe and then bolted across the yard and into the barn in search of Papa. He wasn't there. I raced through and up the ramp out back to spot him high atop the manure pile. I jabbed a finger at the sky and hollered up.

But it wasn't there! Instead only a dark, roiling mass.

"Papa! I saw a horse up there! But it's gone!"

He looked down at me over the pitchfork standing in the dung before him.

"I did! I saw it!" I cried. "But its gone!"

He rubbed at his chin and gave me a slow smile. "Well now. Where do you suppose it went?"

I marveled. "I don't know! It changed!"

Father thought a moment. "Wel-ll now," he drawled. "That's a lesson in there, ain't it. You're gonna find a lot of things change."

. . .

Mama and I had kept up the farm as best we could—with considerable help from members of our parish and the community—but by summer it was sold and passed from our hands. Mama and I moved to Concord to reside with her sister, my Aunt Alice, and I finished my schooling there, though I never recovered what I'd lost with Sunbeam Partridge—at least not until I went to McGill College.

I saw a great deal of both Sophie and Marie in Montreal. And some, too, of Isis, though it became awkward - at least for me. Time and space distanced us, to be sure. But Isis also found a new life; at eighteen or nineteen she married an older gentleman, a Frenchman. She works with young ladies, and with horses, at an exclusive school in Montreal, but has no children of her own. I am unmarried myself and happy for Isis. I confess to wondering that if her years growing up had been different, if they'd been common and there'd never been an occasion for Canada .... or if I'd had more spine or a more expansive heart ... But perhaps I say too much.

One last astonishing thing came about that November of '63. Even as Mama and I returned from Pennsylvania, wagons loaded with building materials had begun making their way up Butternut Mountain. I have never seen it, but another house was put up on the old site down the path. The Drummonds' doing, of course, along with Marie.

And Mama. She had known the project was coming, but kept it to herself til we were home.

Mama still lives in Concord. She goes up to Montreal twice a year, once during the Christmas season and again for a week in the summer. Sophie and Marie have been down several times to New Hampshire to visit her, and two summers ago the four of us went out together to see the old farm. It looks much the same. We spent some time at pleasantries in the kitchen, and I took Sophie and Marie into the barn, where I left them briefly to climb the old stairs and look down into the depths of the hayloft. I saw Isis' head, shorn of its hair. And I heard the echo of my father's voice. *Marty? Is that you up there?*

And it was. It was me.

When I returned, Sophie, now grown tall and gangly, looked at me with hands clasped patiently at her waist.

"Can we go down to Secret Rock now?" she said.

AUTHOR'S NOTE

The characters in this story are fictional creations, though several have basis in fact, principally Lieutenant Edmund Dascomb, who fought with the 2nd New Hampshire Volunteers at Gettysburg. He was wounded there on July 2nd, 1863 and died eleven days later.

While he was home on leave in the Spring of 1862, Edmund traveled about the Granite State giving speeches defending the Union war effort and the Lincoln Administration during the dark days of 1862, when both of these were at a low point. Some of these addresses were reproduced and reviewed in New Hampshire newspapers. Edmund also wrote poetry. In the Military History Museum in Carlisle, Pennsylvania I found a small book of his verse that had been printed in New Hampshire not long after his death. The poem to Marie is entirely of my own creation.

Edmund had a younger sister, Marcia, and an older brother, Milton, a Dartmouth College graduate who went to Mississippi in 1859 and died there shortly after. I have imagined the circumstances of Ned's stay in Louisiana, but the history of the free people of color in New Orleans is well documented.

Lieutenant Dascomb is buried in the Gettysburg National Cemetery, not far below the spot where President Lincoln spoke what I and others think of as the Great American Poem.

ABOUT THE AUTHOR

Ralph Leonard is a career educator with a lifelong interest New England and American Civil War history. He has an MFA in Writing from Vermont College and lives with his wife in Connecticut. Apart from reading and writing, he enjoys bicycling and distance swimming. This is his first work of fiction.

NOTE FROM THE AUTHOR

Word-of-mouth is crucial for any author to succeed. If you enjoyed *Martin Dascomb's Civil War*, please leave a review online—anywhere you are able. Even if it's just a sentence or two. It would make all the difference and would be very much appreciated.

    Thanks!
    Ralph

Thank you so much for reading one of our
Historical Fiction novels.
If you enjoyed our book, please check out our recommendation
for your next great read!

Second Son by Pamela Taylor

"Taylor has done a marvelous job of combining fact, fantasy, and fun."
–IndieReader

View other Black Rose Writing titles at
www.blackrosewriting.com/books and use promo code
PRINT to receive a **20% discount** when purchasing.

Made in the USA
Middletown, DE
14 February 2021